THE ULTRA-VIOLETS
LILAC ATTACK!

WRITTEN BY
SOPHIE BELL

ILLUSTRATED BY
ETHEN BEAVERS

razOr
bill

An Imprint of Penguin Group (USA)

razOr
bill

A division of Penguin Young Readers Group
Published by the Penguin Group
Penguin Group (USA) LLC
345 Hudson Street
New York, New York 10014

USA / Canada / UK / Ireland / Australia / New Zealand / India / South Africa / China
Penguin.com
A Penguin Random House Company

Library of Congress Cataloging-in-Publication Data

Bell, Sophie.
Lilac Attack! / written by Sophie Bell ; illustrated by Ethen Beavers.
pages cm. —(The Ultra Violets ; 3)
Summary: While sixth-grade superheroes Scarlet, Iris, and Cheri are trying to decide if the
formerly evil Opal can be trusted to be an Ultra Violet again, they face a new BeauTek plot,
purportedly to beautify Sync City.
ISBN 978-1-59514-648-9 (hardback)
[1. Superheroes—Fiction. 2. Friendship—Fiction. 3. Good and evil—Fiction. 4. Adventure
and adventurers—Fiction. 5. Science fiction. 6. Humorous stories.] I. Beavers, Ethen,
illustrator. II. Title.
PZ7.B41176Lil 2014
[Fic]—dc23
2013047605

Printed in the United States of America

3 5 7 9 10 8 6 4 2

For Sweetest Nieve*
who brings the Sun
{*that's how we spell it}

Party On
{*As in Roman Numeral 1, Not "Me Me Me"}

"BUT WE JUST *HAD* A PARTY!"

With an impish grin, Scarlet Louise Jones pounded her bare feet in pretend protest across the floorboards of Club Very UV, performing an African Agbekor warrior dance. Which was befitting, becausing she was both the dancer *and* the fighter of the Ultra Violets.

The who, you ask? No, c'mon, be serious, this is book three! *You know*—the Ultra Violets! The fierce trio* of friends transformed into supergirls by an epic sliming of purple goo in a skyscraper FLaboratory when they were seven. That's who!

(*Okay, technically, they're a quartet—or at least they ought to be. There's a fourth supergirl who was touched by the goo, too. But...well, it's complicated. We'll get to her later. Back to the CVUV scene.)

Seated at the black marble table, Iris Grace Tyler looked up from the high-tech, top secret, super-sparkly project she'd been concentrating on. "True," she replied to Scarlet's statement, running one glowing hand through her long purple ringlets, "but that wasn't exactly *our* party. It was Opaline's." (Readers, note: That's her! Opal's the fourth girl!) Iris then proceeded to doodle an entire safari of animals in the air. To decorate Scarlet's dance. "We just hijacked it."

Iris was the artist of the Ultra Violets, and she'd only just begun to discover the depths of her powers. She knew she could create optical illusions out of thin air. And camouflage herself, and beam rainbows, and blast sunrays so hot they'd burn your marshmallows black in seconds flat. At Opal's hijacked birthday party a mere weekend ago, Iris had channeled her solar awesomeness to help reboot their entire short-circuited class.

But this Sunday, with the sixth grade safe and restored to full power, Iris took a break to picture lions and rhinoceroses and giraffes. She blinked her periwinkle eyes for a second or three. And she focused the ultraviolet beams radiating from her fingertips to draw the beasts. Like ancient cave paintings in 3-D, they floated in the air above shorty Scarlet, engoldened by the sunshine streaming through the club's giant flower-blossom window. As Scarlet

2

jumped and spun, her jet-black ponytail whipped right through the drawings, scattering them like glitterdust.

R dems reel tygrrs?

A small skunk with a purple-streaked tail peered suspiciously from his potpourri pillow at Iris's air-drawings.

No worries! Cheri Jeanne Henderson put down her bedazzled blowtorch, pushed up her protective goggles, and skated over from the table to pick up the skunk instead. She gave him a calming pet on the head. *They're no more real than my manicure!*

Cheri always had creatively polished nails. Today, she'd painted dark burgundy stripes across a base coat the color of freshly squeezed orange juice, then topped them with black plastic diamonds. The effect was totally tigeriffic. On platform sandal-skates, she wheeled up to the flower window, the Ultra Violets' mascot in her arms. Darth Odor had been doused by the goo, too, those four years ago in the Fascination Laboratory, aka the FLab. That explained why his stripes were violet, not white. And why he could customize the scent of his spray. (Although, hmmm, that might also have something to do with the time he'd spent caged up in a different lab, the evil Vi-Shush. But . . . well, that's complicated, too!)

The moment they'd set eyes upon each other, even before the *incident de la goo,* Cheri and Darth had bonded. Theirs was a bond deeper than mere words like these! So when one of Cheri's superpowers turned out to be the ability to telepath with animals, it was an added bonus.

"*I'm* still sugar-shocked that everyone saw our superpowers at Opal's party," she said, sliding to a stop beside a vanishing water buffalo. Darth reached out to paw through it. "Or at least they saw both of yours." She pursed her lips to keep from frowning.

Cheri's real Ultra Violet power—her possibly more practical one—was her beautiful mind. Something about the Heliotropium (official name of the purple goo) had turned her brain into a supercomputer, enabling her to run umpteen calculations and solve all sorts of complicated problems using crazy mathtastic formulas that even college graduates didn't understand. It should have been supercool to be superbrilliant. And it was. When Cheri clicked into UV mode, her green eyes gleamed with data streams, and her hair beamed magenta pink. But that was still perhaps a tad subtle compared to Scarlet's power pirouettes or Iris's triple rainbows. Despite Cheri's recent straight As in math, she was, on occasion, a trifle disappointed that her superpowers weren't a little more *sparkly.* If she wanted to be supersmart, she could always just study more, right? Being a superdancer, or a superartist, somehow, sometimes, seemed super*er*...

"The whole class saw us—all three of us, Cher!—in superhero mode," Iris agreed, powering up her hand again and returning her attention to the shiny top secret project on the table. She aimed her pinkie finger at what could have been a sequin. But wasn't. "Which is why this is the perfect opportunity for the Ultra Violets to go all the way public. At the Synchro de Mayo Parade!"

Synchro de Mayo celebrated the founding of SynchroniCity—Sync City, for short—where the girls lived. It was like one big birthday party for all the citizens. And it was happening that very afternoon.

Scarlet stopped dancing long enough to tug up her ankle boots. "Then I guess it's adios, anonymity!" she declared, hitching the slipped strap of her tank top back onto her shoulder. "To the Gazebra?"

At the mention of the place, Cheri broke into giggles. Darth chittered along with her. "Sorry," she explained, tucking a cherry-red strand of hair behind one ear, "but whenever I hear that word, it just makes me think that if a gazelle and a zebra made a baby, that's what they'd call it: a gazebra!"

Darth chittered some more. He did appreciate a good animal joke.

At that very moment, all three of their smartphones binged, and a neon beam burst through the flower window as if the violet band of a rainbow had broken free from all the other colors. Even in the bright midday sun, the silhouette of a violet blossom filled the opposite wall.

"The UV signal!" Cheri gasped, skating back toward the table. Scarlet joined her in a single stag leap. Each girl grabbed her phone.

"'*Weirdness here,*'" Iris read aloud the text they'd all received. "That's all Candace wrote."

"Weirdness?" Scarlet gave a little laugh. "It wouldn't be Sync City without some of that!" The UV spotlight tinted her freckles like flecks on a plum while she tightened her ponytail in preparedness. "Bring it!" she challenged, pumping her fist.

"Girls"—with a last blast of heat from her pinkie finger, Iris put the finishing touches on what was *not* a sequin, nor, for that matter, a rhinestone nor pearl nor paillette—"guess it's time to wing up."

Winging It

Wing up /'wiŋ ' əp/ **(verb): To strap on wings. Prior to flying.**

GLISTENING IRIDESCENT IN THE PALE PURPLE DAYLIGHT, row upon row upon row upon row of the non-sequins covered the tabletop like clothes strewn from the closet of a cabaret singer. Only when Scarlet reached into the spangles and lifted some up did three odd apparatuses start to take shape. Each had padded shoulder straps, same as you'd see on a backpack. Or a parachute. In the center, each had a small square control panel that contained a GPS tracking device, a solar-powered battery with a chargeable electric backup, and a click wheel to adjust angles and speed. And fanning out from both sides of the straps were hummingbird wings.

Robotic ones.

They were made from many delicate layers of circular scales, alternating pieces of wafer-thin vitanium alloy and even thinner, but indestructible, plexi-crystal. (Sequins and paillettes, FYI, are usually just plain old plastic.) Against the black marble of the tabletop, the mechanical wings were almost transparent. But as Iris swung hers on, the crystal discs glinted violet-blue. Scarlet's set gleamed rhinestone gray out to the tips, where the edges deepened to a rich aubergine nearly as dark as her ponytail. And Cheri's, opaque baby-pink at the base, flushed bright fuchsia at the edges.

Scarlet toyed with the controls, her wings flittering to life as she spun the dial. "You're absolutely positive about this, Cher?" she asked.

Cheri nodded, securing Darth in the quilted Kevlar papoose she'd custom-stitched to her set. "Yes, I calibrated each pair to be able to support at least thrice our weights. And Candace says the balance of vitanium and plexi-crystal plates makes the wings both superstrong and superflexible."

Iris gingerly tapped the last few links she'd just soldered onto the frame with her own heat a few minutes ago. Confident they'd cooled, she buzzed up off the ground, her purple corkscrews bouncing behind her and a big smile on her face. Just like real hummingbird wings, the robotic ones vibrated so fast that they were practically invisible—just a blur of violet-blue. "Cher, these are so genius!" Iris exclaimed. "The most viomazing way to make our official Ultra Violet entrance!"

"Well, we did each build our own pair by hand. And the color combinations are your design, RiRi," Cheri said, slightly abashed. "And Scarlet was très good about trying out the prototypes."

Scarlet absentmindedly rubbed her elbow, remembering her many crash tests.

"Yes, but the engineering is all you!" Iris enthused.

Cheri blushed a bit more. "Candace, too," she said modestly.

Candace Coddington, sender of the cryptic text message, beamer of the UV signal, was the girls' erstwhile babysitter and the only witness to the *incident de la goo*. (Depending, you could say she was responsible for it, ahem!) A teenius herself, Candace had completed high school years ahead of schedule.

Now she spent her time taking college classes, assisting the girls' doctor-moms at the FLab, and acting as a mentor to the Ultra Violets. For fun—not even for extra credit, but just because she was forever curious—she had crafted a satellite drone called the MAUVe: an abbreviation for Miniature Aerial Unmanned Vehicle. Then she'd constructed the eco-friendly prismatic cloudship. And now, along with the girls, she'd created the individual robotic hummingbird wings. The cloudship was great for group travel, but wings allowed them to fly solo.

Iris whirred back down in the center of Club Very UV, landing softly on the pink shag rug. Scarlet joined her there, making some final adjustments to the straps around her shoulders and waist. With a quick command to Furi, her smartphone, Cheri uploaded her rollerskate wheels back into the platform heels of her sandals, then skipped over to line up behind her two besties.

"Do you think I need my polka-dot umbrella?" she asked, glancing back over her shoulder to where it sat on the table.

Already halfway up the spiral wrought-iron staircase, Iris looked out the massive flower window, while Scarlet checked a weather app on her phone. "Nah," Scarlet said with a shake of her head. "Looks like blue skies," Iris added. "Purply-blue skies, to me!"

And with that, the Ultra Violets climbed out onto the rooftop of their secret clubhouse.

Instantly the winds whipped through their hair and lifted the many scales of their robotic wingspans. As they rippled against one another, the vitanium and plexi-crystal discs chimed the tiniest tinkling sound, hardly detectable above the gusts. The midday sun powered up the packs. First the girls locked in their target location on the GPS trackers. Then they set the vibration speed to the max. Holding hands, they approached the edge of the roof and . . .

"On the count of three!" Scarlet shouted.

Not daring to look all the way down, they stepped off the building. And out into thin air.

Darth had a slight fear of heights (clouds are not a skunk's natural habitat), so Cheri kept one hand on his papoose as she angled her wings with the other.

Scarlet, hyper as usual, overshot the takeoff and missed slamming into the opposite skyscraper by *thismuch*.

Iris, who was glowing ultraviolet in spite of herself, trailed a slim rainbow behind her as she flew.

In micro-flashes of violet and blue, of crystal and burgundy, of baby pink and bright fuchsia, the Ultra Violets zipped past the windows and between the buildings of Sync, toward the center of the city.

Toward the weirdness.

To the Gazebra.

Powderful Snuff

"LOOOOK, UP IN THE SKY!" DUNCAN MURDOCH MOOED, scratching his stubby cow horns in confusion.

"It's a bird?" the Jensen twins chirped like a chorus, each pointing a skinny finger and lifting a beaky little nose in the air.

"Hel-*lo*, it's *obviously* a plane!" know-it-all Abby O'Adams proclaimed, hands on her hips, although obviously it wasn't.

"It's not a plague of locusts, is it?" Prudence Dosgood whimpered, lacing her fingers under her chin and thinking of all those scary stories from her Sunday school class.

"Or a forward pass?" Brad Hochoquatro planted his feet in a wide stance, prepared to intercept it.

"No," a girl on the edge of the crowd said quietly, her warm chocolate eyes clouded with wisps of milky white. "It's—" But before she could finish her sentence, another boy shouted over her.

"No!" cried Albert Feinstein, captain of the mathletes. He pushed past Brad and Abby and all his other classmates from

Chronic Prep. He pushed up his glasses to get a better view. "It's the Ultra Violets!"

And that boy should know, since by now the Ultra Violets had saved his sorry khaki-covered butt at least twice.

But never mind that, because it *was* the Ultra Violets, wafting down on their glittering iridescent robo-hummingbird wings to the Gazebra at the base of the Highly Questionable Tower, scenically located just alongside the Joan River in Sync City's bucolic Chrysalis Park.

Ultra Violets represent, yay!

As the girls descended, each passed through a dusky lilac beam. From the pilot's seat in the cloudship that she'd strategically drifted above the harbor, Candace pivoted the UV signal, sweeping the searchlight across the crowd.

With a twitch of her lashes, Candace focused the infraviolet zoom lens she'd built into her thick black-framed glasses. She consulted the screen of the tablet computer popped into a slot on the dashboard, scrolling down the

schedule of events. Then she spoke, straightforward and low. The two-way digital microchips she'd embedded in the temple bars of her eyeglasses picked up her voice.

"Here's the deal, girls," she said. "The weirdness is behind you, at the river's edge. But . . ." She paused.

"But?" Iris prompted, talking into her star necklace. The ground was rapidly rising up to meet them.

"But the mayor just announced your arrival," Candace rushed through the words, "so first, it's showtime. Iris, you're clear to fold in your wings. Scarlet, careful not to crash through the boards. Cheri, whoops, wardrobe malfunction: Your skirt's blowing up. Lock it down! Lock. It. Down," Candace directed the three Ultra Violets as they landed. "And . . . cue the glitter blasts," she added, mostly to herself. A quick tap of a vermilion button and showers of shiny confetti squares rained down from the cloudship.

The crowd let out a cheer as the three girls each dropped into place on the podium beneath the black-and-white latticework of the Gazebra. Darth poked his head out of his papoose to admire it. He'd been black-and-purple since he was a baby, but, knowing that skunks and zebras normally shared the same color palette, he approved of the striped design.

Just as Darth gazed up at the Gazebra, Cheri glanced up, up, up to the forty-second floor of the HQT, squinting into the sunlight. She wondered if their doctor-moms were watching them through the rock-crystal windows of the FLab above, or if they were preoccupied, as usual, with some top secret scientific experiment.

Iris didn't squint. The sun, her favorite star, only seemed to give her more power, and she gladly soaked in its warmth. She knew that she was glowing intensely ultraviolet—way brighter than their searchlight. She couldn't help it. And this time, she wasn't trying to hide it. She scanned the throng, past the faces of her classmates, past the citizens of Sync City, searching for just one boy, floating on a hoverboard, a shock of ebony hair falling in his eyes.

But if he was there, she didn't see him.

Scarlet balanced *en pointe* in her biker booties, standing as straight and tall as she could. Not that she'd admit it, even to herself, but she was searching for a boy in the crowd, too. Not Sebastian, Iris's crush. A different boy, one in a black suit jacket and shades that covered his navy blue eyes. One with a salt-and-pepper buzzcut and a sprinkling of freckles.

But she didn't see him, either.

Guess that's no surprise, Scarlet thought, trying to shove Agent Jack Baxter out of her mind. *After all, he is a spy! Hiding is practically his job description.*

If there was a boy in that crowd for Cheri, she hadn't met him yet.

Each Ultra Violet shook off her thoughts as she shook out her hair. A woman was waddling up the podium steps toward them. The girls linked pinkie fingers, and an ultraviolet aura enveloped the threesome.

"Ooh!" Rosenmary Blumesberry, the newly elected mayor of Sync City, cooed in their faces. "Aren't you all just as purply as can be!"

Then she gave Scarlet an impromptu pinch on the nose.

Scarlet's steely gray eyes crossed in surprise and she shot up a half-inch higher, her aubergine ponytail swaying with indignation. It took all her self-control not to grab hold of the mayor's pug nose and tweak back. Hard.

"Stay cool, Scar," Candace's voice crackled in her earpiece. "This new mayor is an unknown quantity; don't overreact."

A squat, square-shaped woman, Mayor Rosenmary Blumesberry had ruddy cheeks and root-beer maroon hair to match. Just the few steps up to the Gazebra had left her sweaty and breathless. Or maybe she was merely excited for the Synchro de Mayo celebrations. Or uncomfortable walking in her pumps—although, with their wide round toes and short stacked heels, they were sensible if not too pretty shoes.

Her back to the crowd, the mayor pulled a fluffy powderpuff from her breast pocket. And dabbed it smack in the center of her face.

"That's better!" she said to the girls with a vigorous sniff, a chalky ring of powder caked across her cheeks. "It's such an effort to keep dry, especially when the sun is so warm and when—"

She paused.

Brushed some stray dust off her shoulders.

And rippled into giggles.

"When," she continued, the crinkles around her eyes now creased with whitish lines of talcum, "you're standing next to a girl giving off heat waves!" She licked a finger and pretended to poke Iris's forehead. "Zszt! Caliente!"

Then, comically clutching her "burnt" hand, Mayor Blumesberry burst into such a titter fit that she doubled over right there on the stage.

Iris exchanged looks with the other two Ultra Violets. Cheri shrugged her shoulders, baffled by the mayor's behavior. Scarlet arched an eyebrow in doubt. This wasn't exactly the official welcome they'd hoped for.

The mayor stayed bent over, hugging her sides and quaking with laughter, her big block W of a booty wiggling at the very citizens who had voted it into office.

From her vantage point in the cloudship, Candace cast a worried eye at the harbor. "Girls, any way to get this back on track?" she asked, just as Scarlet lost patience. Sharply but subtly, she whipped out one leg in a lightning-fast *rond de jambe en l'air*, spinning the mayor around and punting her forward.

"Whooo!" Mayor Blumesberry grasped the Gazebra's podium like she was on an amusement park ride. "Now *that's* what they call a swift kick in the pants!"

". . . *kickinthe pants, kickinthepants, kickinthepants* . . ." Picked up by the podium's microphone, the words broadcast out over the crowd.

"Ah-tee-hee-hem!" The mayor cleared her throat, and that guttural noise growled through the speakers, too. It was impossible to tell whether the woman was at all embarrassed by her blunders: If she was blushing, the crusts of white powder covered it up.

"Citizens of SynchroniCity!" That's how she started, steadying her voice and actually sounding serious at last. "Welcome, on this wonderfully sunny day, to our Synchro de Mayo celebration!"

The crowd whistled and clapped in good cheer, deciding to forget about the previous pants statement.

"Today is my first term of the rest of your lives!" That might have sounded like a threat, if she hadn't said it with such a broad grin. "Our sparkling cosmopolis, SynchroniCity, is a paragon of progress. It leads the way in technological innovation, scientific experimentation, artisanal pickling— the list goes on! That's to say nothing of our museums and theaters and concert halls, and the incredible artists and actors and musicians whose work fills them. We have so much to be proud of!"

Again the crowd applauded, though from up on the Gazebra, Cheri noticed that some of their Chronic Prep classmates had already grown bored of the mayor's speechifying and begun toying with their smartphones instead. Purely by accident her eyes met Albert's. By accident, purely! He was staring right at her, his bottom lip hanging open just a little. Startled, Cheri looked away again. That boy had caused her so much drama!

Bettr iz u avoidz hims, Darth thought, reading her mind.

Absolutely! Cheri agreed. *Avoid him like pleated-front khakis!*

"But, fellow citizens, let's bring it down now," Mayor Blumesberry was saying. "Because it's time to get real. To get really, really real."

The crowd susurrated at this abrupt change in tone, trading worried whispers. Even the Chronic Prep students looked up from their phone screens again. With a staticky *clunk*, Mayor Blumesberry lifted the mic out of its stand and walked with it to the edge of the platform. Interference with the speakers caused a piercing screech. Too late, everyone rushed to cover their ears.

Crouching awkwardly, inching one plump pump forward, then collapsing onto her haunches as she edged out the other, the mayor managed to seat herself on the top step of the Gazebra. She gave the gathering a motherly smile, as if she were reading a story to a circle of kindergartners rather than delivering a speech to an entire city.

"You've heard the rumors," she said in a hush, holding the microphone so close to her mouth she could taste it. "Of three-eyed fish. Day-Glo vegetables. And, yes, of mutants walking these very streets."

Now Mayor Blumesberry had the crowd's complete

attention. The plaza fell so quiet you could have heard a hair split. Duncan Murdoch, suddenly self-conscious, flipped up the hood of his sweatshirt to hide the stumpy horn buds on his head. There'd been so many mutant sightings in Sync City lately that they could no longer be denied, but no politician had ever spoken publicly about them. Until then.

As murmurs ran marathons through the throng, Mayor Blumesberry took the opportunity to tug out her powderpuff again and mop her moist brow. Turning to Scarlet, the Ultra Violet standing closest to her, she whispered, "You girls are so hot!" And gave her a sly wink. Granules of white talc stuck to her eyelashes.

Scarlet wrinkled her nose in response.

"Citizens of Sync City." Sniffling into the microphone, the mayor directed her attention back to the onlookers. "There are indeed rumblings of trouble. And yet . . ."

The crowd leaned forward as one, hanging on the mayor's every word.

". . . there is reason to hope!" she said, struggling to her feet once more. "Some of you Chronic Prepsters may have already witnessed my special guests in action at Tom's Diner."

"Them's my girls!" came a shout from far back. Iris couldn't see who'd said it. But she spotted the top of a towering Oreo-striped bouffant.

"Yes, them's *all* of our girls!" Mayor Blumesberry enthused, echoing the sassy heckler. "Three super sixth-graders are here to keep us safe. To protect Sync City from neon broccoli and whatever other problems may come our way. Right after they finish their homework, *ah-tee-hee-ha!*"

Gripping pinkies tight, the girls braced themselves for Mayor Blumesberry to lose it in another titter fit. Thankfully she held it together.

"So fear not!" she called out. "Or fear less! It probably makes sense to fear just a little. Anyhoo, ladies and gentleman, children and pets, but hopefully NO mutants, without further ado, I present to you . . . the Ultra Violets."

Two Girls, One Boy

"AND LIGHTS . . ." CANDACE DIRECTED, MOSTLY TO herself again, tapping an app on her tablet. Suspended from the cloudship but concealed by its vapors, the power flower began to whirl, its vivid violet beam cutting through the crowd like a lighthouse beacon. "And music . . ." Candace pressed another icon, and a throbbing techno soundtrack started to play. "And Scarlet, you're up."

Like Scarlet needed to be told! She broke away from her two best friends to take center stage on the Gazebra. As Iris and Cheri shimmied and clapped behind her—"Go, Scarlet! Go, Scarlet!"—she launched into a hip-hop ballet solo, mixing classic moves with slammin' swagger with funky chunks of retro disco (to appeal to the senior set) with boot-knocking square dancing (to appeal to the random urban cowboy; Duncan Murdoch, an actual mootant cow boy, got into it, too).

But this wasn't just your average awesome dance mashup. Oh swell no. It was ultraviofied. Scarlet didn't simply perform the steps, she superpowered them, spinning pirouettes at

umpteen times the speed of light, shuffling up and down the Gazebra steps so fast that the Jensen twins got dizzy watching and one of them threw up while Prudence Dosgood wondered if Scarlet was possessed.

The crowd jumped and pumped their fists along with her. They waved their hands in the air like they really *did* care! Scarlet was so in the moment, so in her flow, she practically forgot that anyone else was there. That anything but the music mattered. Her deep purple ponytail hadn't touched her shoulders, and her feet had hardly touched the ground, since she'd started dancing.

As Scarlet grooved, Cheri called out behind her: "The legs were extended at exact ninety degree angles in those cabriole leaps!" And: "That spiraling back flip applied a viostonishing rotational velocity of 989.7 degrees per second!" Her emerald-green eyes glowed with complicated formulas as she supercalculated.

The audience nodded along—Cheri noticed with

dismay that Albert whistled his admiration every time she said a new measurement—but the music was so loud she doubted anyone besides him was listening. People were way more interested in watching breakdancing than hearing a breakdown of it.

C'est la V, she thought the French for "whatever." *No one ever said math was cool. At least not as cool as crunking, alas.*

Math iz cool! Darth thought right back. *2 cool 4 theez fools.*

Cheri lifted the little skunk out of his papoose to cradle him in her arms. *Well, math is the building block of just about everything,* she allowed with a small smile. Her powers might not be as blatantly crowd-pleasing as Scarlet's, but it still felt good to be popular again.

To wrap up her spectacular dance solo, Scarlet threw down a few feats of superstrength. She swung herself around a post completely horizontal, like a flag. She bounced up onto the peak of the Gazebra's shingled rooftop, landing in arabesque. Then she bounded down again and—oh wait:

Traffic jam.

Out on the street.

Scarlet paused in her performance, dashed to the sidewalk, and picked up a double-parked Mister Mushee ice-cream truck. The driver of the car that was wedged in next to it honked his horn in thanks as he pulled out.

She went back to her demonstration, switching Mister

Mushee for Mayor Blumesberry, who was light as a powdered donut in comparison. Scarlet propped her up in the palm of one hand. With the other on her hip, she danced the hora. Aloft, Scarlet's small fingers planted firmly beneath her big butt cheeks, the mayor burst into another titter fit. The loud music swallowed the sound of her laughter, but the crowd could still see her jiggling like a rosy Jell-O mold.

"Okay, Scarlet, nailed it!" Candace stated from her aerial observation point. "Superpowers officially public. Iris, you're up next!"

Scarlet put the mayor down. Gave a quick curtsy. And spun around. With her back to the crowd and her arms flung wide open, she mega–stage dove off the Gazebra to the *ka-swish!* of a last glitter blast. The force of her thrust propelled her all the way to the edge of the audience. Buoyed by her classmates, she bodysurfed up to the mosh pit. When finally she dropped onto two feet, she shouted, "Go, Iris!" punching her fist in the air.

"Go, Iris," she barely heard the girl beside her say.

As the mosh pit pushed and pulled with the rhythm, Scarlet whipped her head around to find herself nose-to-nose with Opaline Trudeau.

The smile left Scarlet's face, but she didn't look away. The last time she'd been this close to Opal, the rogue supergirl had pulled her hair. Instinctively, Scarlet now brushed her burgundy-black bangs out of her eyes. Tiny squares of glitter that had nestled in the strands sprinkled down, one landing on her cheek, others clinging to the damp skin of her bare shoulder. For the second time since the Synchro de Mayo festivities started, all the chaos around her seemed to fall away. Scarlet felt as if it were just she and Opaline, standing in a rollicking sea of strangers, trying to find their balance.

"Hi, Scarlet," Opal said, her eyes cast downward. She seemed, Scarlet thought, embarrassed. Shy, like she used to be.

Scarlet didn't answer right away. She realized she was clenching her fists at her sides.

"Viomazing dance," Opal mumbled, bumping into her (purely by accident) as the crowd surged forward like a wave.

"You're not planning on electrocuting anyone, are you?" Scarlet snapped. The anger in her own voice took her by surprise.

"Oh, no!" Opal stammered, shrugging into herself. "I'm off-duty."

If that was supposed to be a joke, Scarlet wasn't laughing.

"You'd better not be wearing that poison perfume, either!" she warned.

Opal just shook her head and offered Scarlet a feeble smile. Although her brunette bob was already pinned back with barrettes, she tucked her hair behind her ears anyway.

Scarlet stared harder. Even in the bright Sunday sun, bathed by the beam of the Ultra Violet searchlight, she could see the electric volts sparking off Opal's shoulders. Opal couldn't hold her gaze. As she blinked back and forth at Scarlet, milky white clouds passed across her brown eyes. Scarlet debated threatening her. Telling her to leave the Gazebra ASAP. Sugarsticks, if she so chose, Scarlet could just pick up Opal, who was umpteen times lighter than an ice-cream truck, and pitch her into the river!

But she didn't.

With great power comes great responsibility, Scarlet thought. She'd heard that somewhere before. Suddenly she understood what it meant.

"I'm watching you," was what she said instead. "We all are."

"Okay!" Opal called after her as Scarlet began to make her way back to the Gazebra's stage. "Later!"

Scarlet wasn't sure how to read Opal's tone, and she refused to turn around and meet her eyes again. The crowds parted as she passed, clapping along, and soon all the noise washed over her once more. Shaking off the encounter,

Scarlet sprung a few feet off the ground every few steps, high-fiving her fans.

Opal hung back, letting her go.

But someone else followed close behind, weaving in and out of the crowd in Scarlet's wake. Camouflaged in an Average Joe disguise of cargo shorts and graphic tee, he nearly blended in with the rest of the Chronic Prep kids—which he wasn't. And he stood short enough that he easily could have ducked behind some grown-up's mom jeans if Scarlet had actually bothered to look back—which she didn't. Even if she had, it would have been hard to recognize his face behind his black sunglasses.

Though she probably would have spotted his salt-and-pepper hair.

V*

Fringe Elements
{*Because the Roman Numeral for 5 Looks a Lot Like V for Violet}

SPEAKING OF CAMOUFLAGE...

Up on the stage of the Gazebra, Iris's superpower demonstration was in full swing.

First she'd painted a rabble of rainbow butterflies using just one pinkie, twirling around as she set each gauzy-winged illusion aflight.

Then she'd pretty much turned *herself* into a rainbow, shooting the full color spectrum from her fingertips and filtering it from her pale blue eyes through her purple lashes. If the citizens of Sync City had any fears about the mutants Mayor Blumesberry had mentioned just a few minutes ago, Iris's happy rainbow blitzkrieg blew them from their minds for the moment. With Iris's intense high beams bouncing off the carved crystal walls of the HQT and refracting into a million *more* rainbows, all of them tinted violet whenever the power flower searchlight swooped past, the scene in Chrysalis Park could have been a time warp to an old, turn-of-the-twentieth-century dance party known as a rave.

Now Iris concentrated all her beams back into herself, unifying the colors until all that remained was the whitest ultraviolet, radiating out of every pore. She blazed so bright she looked like a star herself—not the Hollywood type, though she probably did look like that, too, but the diamond-in-the-sky type, come down to earth. Everyone in the crowd *ooh*ed and *ahh*ed and blinked and squinted and had to scramble to put on their sunglasses.

Cheri had tried to narrate Iris's performance by describing the viomazing math behind each part—announcing the average distance traveled by a migrating monarch butterfly, explaining that a rainbow was made up of angular 42-degree radii—that kind of stuff. But she gave up again around the time when all the gawkers were fumbling for their sunglasses. As had happened during Scarlet's act, once more Cheri realized that the audience just wanted to *experience* Iris's color explosions, not listen to a lecture about them. And once more Cheri was an *itsy* bit bothered by her super-BFFs' flagrant power plays, even though she knew that was the whole point of this coming-out party.

What she *knew* was one thing. What she *felt* was another. You know?

So as Iris sparkled on, Cheri, every now and then, would traipse across the stage holding up Darth. He'd let rip with some wonderfully aromatherapeutic scent that the whole crowd clamored to inhale, *mmm*ing and *ahh*ing even deeper.

Cher was glad everyone was into the Ultra Violet skunk—even if she did feel like one of those game show hostesses whose only role was to spin a giant wheel or flip around letters on a great big board.

I'm getting great big bored myself! she mused.

Snuggling Darth close, she scanned the crowd for Scarlet, who had disappeared after her mega–stage dive.

Whaz iz she drownded? Darth thought, alarmed.

Cheri stroked the bridge of his nose. *No worries, it wasn't that type of dive,* she reassured the fretful skunk. *Anyway, Scarlet's so strong, I bet she could swim with sharks.*

Sharks on her mind, Cheri glanced past the black-and-white posts of the Gazebra, down the grassy lawn to the river. A curious party—of picnickers?—caught her eye. And made her skin crawl.

They stood in a semicircle at the water's edge. From behind, they all looked eerily similar. *Members of the same family?* Cheri wondered. Taking in their strange outfits, she thought they must have been part of a tour group from another country. Or planet. *Or maybe they're wearing costumes for the Synchro de Mayo celebrations,* she reasoned. Though already she didn't believe that.

Each one sported a long grass skirt, like you'd wear to a luau, with a loud floral-print shirt on top. Cheri couldn't tell if they were dancing or chanting or what, but every so often they would toss handfuls of pollen-yellow something into

the harbor. *Flowers?* Cheri guessed. From that distance she couldn't be sure. And the scent that wafted back on the wind was anything but sweet. It reminded her of rotting vegetables wrapped in dirty laundry.

"Ahchoopsie!" she discreetly sneezed, dabbing her watering eyes with the tip of Darth's tail. Maybe Iris's heat waves were taking a toll on her after all. She felt just a little bit sick.

I must be seeing double, she told Darth, blinking. The closer she peered, the more the tourists' arms looked like sticks: thin, brittle, blackish. And in quadruplicate. With a melting ice-cream cone clasped in at least one of their four hands.

Dat be odd, Darth observed.

"That," Cheri murmured back, "be weirdness."

Out in the audience, after Opal lost sight of Scarlet, she focused her attention on Iris's viomazing light show. *Hope*

Sync City remembered to wear sunblock today! she thought wryly as Iris's ultraviolet rays blazed across the crowd, surely sunburning the tops of any bald heads they touched. Opal tugged on her cuffs, pulling them down until her hands were almost hidden inside her long sleeves. But only from anxiousness. Not because she had any concerns about UV radiation. After all, she had been doused in the Heliotropic goo same as her three former besties lo those four years ago. Her DNA had been altered, too. It was why she had superpowers just like the other Ultra Violets.

Yes, you read right: the *other* Ultra Violets. That's exactly what Opal thought. Because despite everything that had gone down between them, all the Albert drama, the mutant foofaraw, the hijacked birthday party . . .

Despite all that . . .

Opaline Trudeau still considered herself an Ultra Violet.

But Scarlet Jones definitely doesn't, Opal thought, based on the tense encounter they'd just had. *And by now Cheri Henderson has probably calculated some brilliant algebraic formula to negate my "fundamental ultravioletness" or something!* Opal crossed her arms, her hands still tucked up inside her sleeves. The cuffs hung empty at her elbows. *Iris Tyler used to think I was an Ultra Violet, though.* She remembered how Iris had hugged her right there in the park, just before her notorious birthday. *Wonder if there's any chance she still does.*

Iris's ultraviolet beams could burn in a fight—Opal had felt their heat. And Opal's lightning bolts could shock—she'd blasted Iris off her feet. When their hug took a turn for the wrong, the two of them had nearly combusted! But, it suddenly occurred to Opal, maybe, since they shared the same altered genes, neither girl could ever really destroy the other.

Because that would be like destroying yourself—or would it?

It was the kind of scientific question Opal might have asked Candace, her erstwhile babysitter and volunteer fairy godmother. If only the two were still on speaking terms.

Opal sighed, heart and head heavy with all these thoughts, as she stood there in the thick of the ridiculously blissful crowd celebrating Synchro de Mayo and the Ultra Violets' coming-out. The audience loved the supergirls! Iris hadn't even had to zombotomize their Chronic Prep class to get them to clap along to her light show.

Opal's gaze drifted across the sea of spectators, coming to rest on a boy. His back was turned to her, but that was almost always how she looked at him anyway. At his shaggy sandy hair and the tips of his pinkish earlobes peeking out from underneath. "Feinstein" came far before "Trudeau" in the alphabet; Opaline almost always sat rows behind Albert in class.

As if he could sense the power of her stare pressing

against the back of his neck, Albert twisted around and their eyes met. But just for a second. Then both of them quickly looked away.

What else did I expect? Opal felt a twinge for her old crush in the pit of her stomach. *I never went out on that chess date with him. And I did short-circuit his brain.* She would have laughed if it weren't all such a mess. To this day, Albert had zero idea of the devastating impact he'd had on the four girls' friendships. *So smart*, Opal thought, risking another glimpse in the direction of the mathlete captain, *and yet so clueless*.

With another small sigh, Opal returned her attention to Iris. She began to imagine what *she* would do, how *she* would show off, if she were up on that Gazebra with the other three . . .

A swaggery voice broke into her daydreams.

"'Sup, girl?"

Swan Jive

A HUSKY BOY WITH CRINKLED ORANGE HAIR AND flushed cheeks to match was standing uncomfortably close to Opal, waiting for her answer. In one plump hand he clutched two defenseless hot dogs; the other held a sweaty can of soda. Grinning, he chomped off the ends of his frankfurters—both of them in one bite. "I'm in training," he said, as if that excused his piggishness. "Defending my title this afternoon." Opal could smell the sour relish on his breath. She could see the crusts of yellow mustard in the corners of his mouth.

Opal leaned back. Keeping her arms crossed, she looked him up and down. But she didn't recognize the boy from Chronic Prep.

"Do I know you?" she asked, her voice clipped with suspicion.

"Depends," the boy said before washing down his masticated hot dogs with a slurp from his soda. "What's your name?"

Opal bit her lower lip, but the question was so direct she didn't know how to avoid it. "Opaline," she reluctantly admitted.

"Opaline!" the boy boomed right back to her. Sometimes people stumbled over her name, because it wasn't the most common. But the way this boy said it was as if he'd known it all along. As if he was just waiting for a chance to show it off. "Call me Sid," he ordered. "And now, yeah, you know me."

"Sid" went to extend a hand before remembering that both were filled with junk food. As Opal watched, appalled, the boy shrugged, then tucked the remains of the two helpless hot dogs under his armpit. He stretched out his now-empty palm.

Opal cringed at the sight of the five greasy fingers wriggling toward her. Just a week or so ago, she would have shocked this kid on the spot without a second thought. But somehow, basking in the secondhand glow of the Ultra Violets' performance, she wasn't sure what to do. Tentatively

40

she snaked a hand out from its hiding place in her sleeve. Sid's immediately pounced on it, pumping her arm up and down like a jump rope. His hand was so large it completely swallowed hers. She could feel the lingering bready dampness of the buns that had gone before her and was filled with a weird rush of sympathy for the squished hot dogs.

Gritting her teeth, she yanked free her hand.

"So how about this whole scene?" Sid elbowed her roughly in the shoulder. "Like, supergirls in Sync City? That's k-ray-z, right?" He wiped his hand down the front of his shirt, rubbed it through his frazzled carrot hair, then retrieved his half-eaten hot dogs from his armpit.

"Um, right," was all Opal mumbled in response. "Crazy." She tried to look past him, to some escape route out of this awkward conversation, but the boy tilted in too close. She couldn't see a thing beyond the ketchup stain on his collar.

Someone seriously needs to teach this Sid kid the concept of personal space, Opal thought, squirming backward and folding in her arms again. The sharp threat of a headache throbbed at her temples, and her vision began to blur.

"And mutants?" he pressed, hovering over her. "What's *that* about?"

Opal glared sideways at the red-faced boy. This wasn't a conversation; it was an interrogation.

"Yeah. Scary," she deadpanned, watching his face for a reaction.

"I don't suppose *you've* ever seen a mutant, have you,

41

Opaline?" He sounded out her name as if it were another deep-fried snack for him to devour. She imagined the letters mixing with the relish and rubbery hot dogs already in his mouth. The idea made her queasy. "Any mutants at your school, *Opaline?*" he persisted, poking her again with his pudgy elbow. It reminded her of how teachers sometimes talked to you, or salespeople in stores. Using your name like they're trying to help you, like they're on your side, when really they're trying to trap you, or sell you something you don't need. Opal had just met this kid. He didn't have the right to roll out her name like he owned it! They weren't friends. In fact, she was starting to hate him.

She locked onto his hazel eyes, knowing by now that hers must have been spiraling with white. As Sid stared back at her, he began to wobble, losing his balance.

"Have I ever seen a mutant?" Opal repeated his question back at him. Maybe she would tell him she'd once commanded a battalion of them—as if! "Well, *Sid*"—it was a short name, so she couldn't drawl it out anywhere near as long as he had hers, but she did the best she could, then mocked him with his own words from before—"that 'depends.' You look like *you* might be a mutant. In which case, yeah, I guess I have seen one."

Opal could tell instantly that her answer angered the big red boy. He choked a bit on the bun in his mouth, crumbs sticking to the dried-up mustard at the corners. The flush on his cheeks flared into a five-alarm fire. With her hands still sheathed inside her sleeves, Opal pinched the soft under-skin of her forearms to stop herself from smirking. Any second now, she bet, this blubbery volcano was going to blow.

"Agent Bristow." A low, insistent voice came between them. "No fraternizing. With the, uh, civilians. Remember, dude?"

"But she's *not* a civilian!" Sid protested, turning toward his friend and forfeiting the staring contest. "She's—"

Before Opal could hear just what, according to this boy, she was, his buddy gave him a friendly (?) punch in the stomach.

"Oof!" Sid blurted, coughing up the remains of his hot dogs. He slapped a hand across his mouth, stickily shoving them back in, then took a long swig from his soda. But he must have sucked in some air—purely by accident—because he began coughing harder.

While Sid spluttered and hacked, Opal sized up the other boy. He was a lot shorter than his friend. *Almost as short as Scarlet Jones*, Opal couldn't help thinking. He had a smattering of freckles like Scarlet, too. But while Scarlet's licorice-black locks shone aubergine when she was in Ultra Violet mode, this boy was graying at the temples of his short, clean-edged haircut.

That's different, Opal noted, even though it did give the boy a serious vibe that was sort of cool.

At last "Agent Bristow" got it together. He must have been pretty embarrassed by his friend punching him in the stomach, especially considering that his friend was a pipsqueak. Opal fought another impulse to smirk.

"Anyway," Red Sid said, his voice still raspy from coughing, "I thought you were supposed to be trailing the—"

This time the short boy stomped on the big kid's foot.

"Youch!" he yelped, hopping up and down. "Baxter, what the—"

"Soda. Makes him hyper," the boy with the salt-and-pepper hair bluntly explained as he ushered Sid into the crowd. "Sorry. To bother you. Opaline."

Opal's eyebrows shot up. It was bad enough she'd actually told the big red one her name. But how did the lil' freckled one already know it?

Bristow and Baxter, she repeated. *I know your names now, too.*

An urge overtook her, and this time she didn't resist. She freed one hand from its sleeve and, pointing her pinkie finger, whipped a thin lightning bolt through the bystanders.

"Yowza!" Agent Bristow howled, reaching back to cover his zapped butt as his crinkled orange hair stretched out straight.

Bull's-eye! Opal thought, smugly holstering her electric hand again.

But we were speaking of camouflage, weren't we? That was so one chapter ago! That was where the chapter BEFORE this one began. And it's where Iris was ending her performance. Gradually she dimmed her ultraviolet diamond light, fading it out in disintegrating glitter-dusted beams. Like a *star*set, instead of a sunset. (Though, since the sun *is* a star, they're actually the same thing.) The crowd *ahh*ed and *ooh*ed once more, now fumbling to pluck off their sunglasses so that they could see every last sparkle. And as they watched, they realized it wasn't only the light beams that were vanishing. No, the purple-tressed Ultra Violet herself seemed to be disappearing right before their eyes!

"She's invisible!" someone cried, though that wasn't 100 percent true. Iris was just camouflaging herself—blending in, like a chameleon, with the black-and-white stripes of the Gazebra. Only her periwinkle blue eyes and glints of her royal purple ringlets remained.

This has gone viomazingly! Iris thought, sneaking up to the steps of the stage and peering out at the audience. It was funny to watch them craning their necks to find her when she was standing right in front of them. Iris allowed herself a small smile of satisfaction. *Scarlet was fierce*, she reflected, *Cher was brill, and everyone seemed to love my light show!* It had been Iris's idea for the Ultra Violets to come out. But on the inside, she'd been pretty nervous about it. What if all of Sync City had decided they weren't superheroes after all, but superfreaks? What if, instead of clapping, they'd booed and thrown moldy peaches and demanded their money back—even though the performance was free? Worse, what if they'd been arrested?

Standing before an adoring crowd might have been a strange time to think so pessimistically, but Iris's mind moved in mysterious ways. She'd never forgotten what Candace once said about people who might want to probe them like specimens. Scarlet had gulped and Cheri had whimpered.

Opal was still with us then, Iris recalled. That night, she had tried to calm down her three BFFs. But what if Candace had been right? (She usually was.) What if there WERE people who still wanted to probe them? Now that *everybody* knew . . .

Even in the warmth of the afternoon sun, even with her own solar heat radiating from every single one of her chemically altered cells, Iris shuddered with a sudden chill. Out of the corner of her eye, she caught sight of Mayor Blumesberry, way off by the Mister Mushee truck. To Iris's shock, the woman was absorbed in a conversation with none other than Develon Louder! She was covering her face with her black Burkant pocketbook, but Iris recognized the president of BeauTek instantly. Because who else hid behind their designer handbag like that?! As Develon ranted, her silver chignon slid around like a loose scoop of ice cream atop her head. Mayor Blumesberry nodded along, anxiously wringing the powderpuff between her hands. And now, as far as Iris could see, she wasn't tittering one bit.

Same As It Ever Was?

FOR BETTER AND FOR GOOD. FOR PINKER AND FOR purpler. In sunshine and in sparkliness. The Ultra Violets had come out. You can't put a rainbow back in a pot! (Any leprechaun worth his gold knows that.) With a series of *coupés jetés en tournant*, Scarlet joined Cheri on the Gazebra's stage just as Iris was returning to her normal colors.

"And . . . link pinkies," Candace instructed from on high. "And . . . do the wave . . ." The girls did a mini-wave, Darth bringing up the rear with a swish of his tail. "And . . . Handshake Dance . . ." The girls performed their original, with the booty shake and bunny hop. "And . . . take a bow."

Blasts of confetti rained down on them as they did.

Afterward, the trio took their Walk of Fame through the throng, mingling with the citizenry. They shook hands and kissed babies and got photo-bombed and signed autographs until Scarlet's cheeks hurt from smiling and Cheri ran out of lip gloss to reapply and all of Iris's glitter pens ran dry.

"Candace, what's the status?" Iris asked, casually speaking toward the microphone in her necklace. "What about the weirdness—should we go investigate that now?"

"The weirdness went underground while you guys were rocking the plaza," Candace said cryptically. "We'll have to circle back to it, 'cause I'm late for my shift at the FLab."

"Um, okay," Iris hesitated. She'd wanted to tell Candace her concerns about the mayor, but not there in the middle of the square, where anyone might hear. And really, it was just a feeling. But Iris was an artist: She valued feelings above everything else. Fortunately, Candace was all about the gut-check, too. They'd talk. Maybe not right now, but soon.

"Then we can go?" Scarlet asked, cupping her Tooth Fayree earpiece to block out the sounds of the festival around them.

"You girls have more than earned the rest of the afternoon off." Candace's voice crackled over the microchip microphones. "So, yes, make like bananas and split!"

Cheri giggled at the joke. It just made Scarlet realize how famished she was. As they wended their way out of Gazebra Plaza, they hit up as many of the Synchro de Mayo food stands as they could handle. Tacos and falafels, popcorn and cotton candy, strawberry smoothies and chocolate milkshakes: Now that they were official supergirls, the chefs gave them everything for free.

"Our first perks!" Cheri gushed, feeding a piece of caramel corn to Darth. "Awesome!" Darth would have clapped, too, if his paws hadn't been hugging a roasted peanut.

"We're going to be saving this city from who knows what," Scarlet said with a puckish grin. "So if people want to comp us some dang burritos, then *gracias*, I say!"

Snacks in bags, Darth snug in his papoose, and robo-hummingbird wings activated, the three girls buzzed up into the air. As they flew alongside the Joan River promenade en route to their favorite place in Chrysalis Park, the late-day sun gave their vitanium-crystal wings an ethereal aura. If you didn't know they were superheroes, you just might have mistaken them for angels. Angels with hot pink, electric blue, and deep burgundy wings.

Down by the Gazebra, Opaline Trudeau stood alone, her open face tilted skyward. She watched the Ultra Violets go with what could only be described as . . . longing.

She wasn't the only one watching. Or longing. Though the skinny, black-haired boy balancing on his hoverboard at the outskirts of the scattering crowd only had eyes for one Ultra Violet. Until that afternoon, he hadn't even known she was an Ultra Violet. He hadn't even know what an Ultra Violet was! He just knew her as Iris. He just thought she was the sweetest, coolest girl he'd ever met. And now he wondered what he could ever do to impress her—and if he even knew her at all.

. . .

"I saw Opal."

Scarlet waited until they'd touched down atop the grassy knoll, spread out their freebie picnic, and she had at least one dang burrito in her belly before sharing the news.

"OMV, no way," Iris said from her seat on the bench. She really should have been eating something more nutritious than cotton candy, but she wasn't. The sticky pink strands of spun sugar that she'd pinched between her fingertips floated in the breeze. "You saw her in the crowd?"

"Yup." Scarlet swallowed the first bite of burrito numero two.

"How did she look?" Cheri demanded. "What was she wearing? Was she still angry about her birthday? Who else was she with? What did she say?"

"Umm . . ." Scarlet dug a heel into the dirt, trying to sort out all those questions in her head. "I wasn't super paying attention to her outfit."

"What!" Cheri cried, crushed. That would have been the first thing she'd notice! It was possibly the main thing she was interested in. Frowning, she propped herself up on her elbows.

"Well, *excusez-moi*, Cher, I guess I was too distracted by the possibility of her *striking* the Gazebra with *lightning!*" Scarlet shot back in her own defense. "She looked like Opal, okay? The collar. The barrettes. A dress, I think. With knee socks. Is that enough of a runway report for you?"

"What kind of dress?" Cheri pressed her luck. "Was it straight up and down, like a sheath? Or did the skirt flare out in an A-shape? Or—"

Scarlet's exasperated stare stopped Cheri from listing any more style options.

After a slightly awkward pause, Iris tried to kickstart the conversation again. "Did she make any threats, Scar?" she asked, passing her the bucket of popcorn. "What *did* she say?"

With her head down, Scarlet picked out just one piece of popcorn, inspecting it like it was some precious gem. "She said my dance was 'viomazing,'" she muttered.

"It totally was!" Cheri declared immediately, hoping to smooth over their spat.

"Thanks," Scarlet said, giving Cheri a playful eyeroll as she chucked the popcorn into her mouth. "But it was weird to hear Opal say it. To hear her say 'viomazing.'"

"No kidding," Iris agreed. "That's UV-speak."

"She cheered for your light show, too," Scarlet reported.

"Huh." Iris twirled another strand of cotton candy between her fingertips. "That's . . . interesting. Do you think she was trying to fool you?"

"If she was, I wasn't buying it. I warned her we were watching."

Iris nodded. "Good. I guess we really do have to stay vigilant now. All the time," she added ruefully. "About everything." The ginormousness of their responsibilities hit her all at once. "Yikes?" To protect an entire city from every single threat seemed so impossible as to be absurd. She started laughing softly.

"Yet here we are having a picnic!" Cheri exclaimed, sweeping an arm out over their little street-fair feast. Beside her, Darth did the same to his tiny pile of pretzels and crushed potato chips.

"Hey, we have to keep our energy up," Scarlet said, unapologetic. "That was some crazy matinee we just threw down!" She snapped a chocolate chip cookie in half to split with Darth. "Anyway," she continued, "the new Opal reminded me of . . . the old Opal. All quiet and shy. I just don't know if it was an act."

Cheri took a sip from her strawberry smoothie before speaking. "Or maybe she finally ate some mumble pie."

"Some what?" Iris said, beginning to giggle again.

"Mumble pie," Cheri repeated, tearing off a handful of cotton candy for herself. "That's what they say when you've learned your lesson and you act all embarrassed and mumbly about it."

Scarlet stared at her friend, dumbfounded. "No, Cher, you mean *humble* pie," she corrected. "*That's* the expression!"

"Really?" Cher knit her eyebrows together in doubt. "Are you sure? Doesn't *mumble* kind of make more sense?"

"Mumble pie is what the mutants are going to eat when I punch their teeth out!" Scarlet shouted, springing fifteen feet off the ground in a cheerleading X jump. Clearly the burritos were helping her refuel.

Maybe the stress of coming out in public was catching up to Iris. Maybe she was feeling washed out from her spectacular light show. Whatever! Either way, she was laughing so hard by now that she wasn't even making a sound. Pale ultraviolet tears ran down her cheeks. As soon as she wiped them away, fresh ones took their place. "Mumble pie or humble pie," she gasped, "as long as it's à la mode, count me in!" Then she started crying with laughter again.

Cheri chuckled, too, waiting for Iris to calm down. At long last she did, and the three girls lapsed into a comfortable silence. Iris lay back on the bench and looked up at the clouds while Scarlet twirled *chaîné* turns in a circle around the hilltop and Cheri fashioned a buttercup crown for Darth. She didn't mind if her slips of the tongue made the other two giddy. Scarlet had said they needed to keep their energy up: Cheri figured they needed to keep their spirits up, too. If that meant laughing at her flubs . . .

Then *c'est la V!* she philosophized. Goofs aside, she was still the superbrain of the group. Iris could be ultra sensitive.

And Scarlet could turn ultra furious in a flash. *One* of the threesome had to keep a level head.

U shud telz dem, Darth urged, nibbling on his cookie crumbs.

Cheri combed her fingers down the skunk's soft tail.

"It's awesome everyone was so into us today," she said out loud. "Or at least into you two. I don't think anyone was especially blown away by my brainpower, alas!"

"Cher, that's so not true!" Iris objected, sitting up straight. "And if it is, well . . . no offense to them, but the citizens are kind of clueless."

"The ultimate oblivios," Scarlet piped in as she pirouetted past them.

"Math skills may not be as sparkly as rainbows . . ." Iris smiled sheepishly.

"Or as funky as crunking!" Scarlet shouted, hip-hopping by again.

"But we wouldn't be the Ultra Violets minus them," Iris finished.

Cheri smiled back, then took a deep breath. "Okay, because I've been thinking about equations again. Chemical equations."

Iris hugged her knees to her chest now, listening, as Scarlet spun to a stop and flopped down on the grass opposite her. "*And* so ends my oh-so-brief vacation to my happy place!" Scarlet groused.

"Sorry." Cher grimaced. "It's nothing specific, it's just, if BeauTek manufactured more than the test quantity of mind-control chemicals like the ones in Opal's perfume—"

"That I burned up at her party," Iris said.

"Yes," Cheri continued. "If there's more, BeauTek might have to use it soon, while the ingredients are still active. Once chemicals are combined, they can deteriorate or destabilize fast. "

"Like a use-it-or-lose-it situation?" Scarlet asked. Iris didn't say anything; she just thought about Opal, and moldy peaches, again. About how something delicate and sweet could turn dark and rotten overnight.

"Precisely." Cheri dug a bottle of biodegradable nail polish out of her pocket and held it up to the light. Its rosy purple sequins had drifted to the bottom; a layer of clear lacquer sat on top. "This color is called Lilac Attack," she said as an aside. "Don't nail polishes always have the funniest names?" She gave the bottle a few brisk shakes, mixing the components together again. "Anyway, when I was standing there on the Gazebra stage while you two were being fabulous," she said, "I caught a whiff of something foul. Not even Darth's squirts could cover it up."

Scarlet had plucked a yellow dandelion from the grass and was tugging off its petals. "I didn't smell it when I was bodysurfing," she said. "And I asked Opal right to her face if she was wearing her poison perfume, but she denied it!"

"I didn't smell anything, either," Iris mused. "Maybe the heat from my solar rays burned it off before it could reach my nose? But as for BeauTek . . . Okay, I have no idea what they were saying, but I saw Develon Louder talking to the mayor."

Scarlet's jaw dropped open and a piece of popcorn tumbled out.

"The mayor was beaucoup kooky," Cheri said, painting a fresh layer of lilac sequins on her thumbnail. "What was up with that powderpuff?"

"If I was about to announce to an entire city that they were under threat of a mutant attack, I'm not sure I'd be all giggly about it." Iris twined a long purple ringlet around her pinkie finger, then let it unravel. "Though I guess I sort of just was?"

"That's different," Scarlet countered. "We're alone here. And we needed to 'decompress,' as my mom always says when she gets home from work."

Iris was winding up the same ringlet again. "True." She sighed. "I guess I just hoped that going public might make things a little easier."

"But obvi Develon and BeauTek are still whipping up who-knows-what," Scarlet said.

"Opal's still a question mark," Iris added.

"And Mayor Blumesberry's an even bigger one!" Scarlet snorted.

"Maybe not much has changed," Cheri deduced.

"Same as it ever was?" Iris wondered. She released the ringlet and held out her pinkie. The other two girls leaned in for a quick tap. The ultraviolet burst that flared up from their fingertips reflected in their eyes. "We trust Candace," Iris concluded. "And that's it."

Blindsided

YES, ONE OF THE MANY THINGS THE ULTRA VIOLETS had learned during this sparkly superhero gig thus far was that trust had to be earned. Truly has there ever been a truer truism? Their erstwhile babysitter had seen them through thick, thin, perfume, mutants, and goo (not necessarily in that order), so she topped the trustworthy list.

For just about everyone else, the data was inconclusive.

Were that trust was a solid! But trust's state of matter—if ever this comes up on a science test, FYI—was closest to a gas: constantly shifting, hard to get your hands around, and highly flammable.

Two out of three Ultra Violets were about to feel the burn.

Sebastian Fassbender had tried to follow Iris Tyler as she flew away from Gazebra Plaza on her robo-hummingbird wings. But his hoverboard, while hydraulic, wasn't as swift, and whenever he'd looked up into the sky to find her, he'd just ended up blinded by the sun. Now he found himself alone on the riverside promenade of Chrysalis Park, performing little tricks on his board and debating what to do next. Even if he did venture deeper into the park and cross paths with Iris, what would he say to her? He didn't know how he felt about her being an "Ultra Violet," as the mayor had called them. And that was another thing: No doubt Iris would be hanging out with her two best friends. No way could he talk to her in front of them!

He pushed the shaggy black forelock out of his eyes. Then he jumped his hoverboard up onto the top rail of the latticed Plexiglas fence that bordered the Joan River, and glid (*that's how we spell it*) sideways down the length of it until he nearly lost his balance and had to bail back onto the orange brick path. He was just picking up his board and checking it for scratches when he noticed two boys approaching. The duo was a study in opposites, one plump and sort of egg-shaped, with a tussock of frizzy orange hair, the other short, compact, and clean-cut. The bigger one toted what might have been a basketball under his arm. The lil'er one had his hands shoved into the pockets of his shorts. It took Sebastian a moment to recognize them. The last time he'd seen the two boys, they'd both been in black suits. And trapped in a fluffula tree. The runt had been hanging upside down.

"Way to almost wipe out, bro!" the big kid mocked. As he came closer, Sebastian could see he was wearing a blue satin sash with SYNCHRO DE MAYO HOT-DOG-A-PALOOZA—1ST PLACE WIENER! printed across it in white letters. He realized it wasn't a basketball after all that the boy was carrying, but a bucket of fried chicken.

"Drumstick?" the kid offered, holding one out in his oily fist.

"I'm good, thanks," Sebastian declined. Although his mother had never specifically told him *not* to accept fried chicken from strangers, it still seemed like a sketchy idea.

The three boys stood there awkwardly, Sebastian holding his hoverboard in front of him like some sort of shield, the red-haired kid gnawing on the drumstick he'd just passed up, and the lil' one, tight-lipped beneath his dark sunglasses, shifting his weight from foot to foot.

"You guys skate?" Sebastian said at last, because it seemed like somebody was supposed to say something— and he didn't think the two boys would want him to bring up how he'd rescued them from a fluffula tree like a couple of stranded kittens.

"Oh, definitely, all the time," the big one boasted. "But not really. My build is better for football. Or wrestling. You know—contact sports."

The short kid gave a sharp laugh at this. His friend scowled down at him, cheeks pinkening. "Shut up, Baxter," he muttered.

"How 'bout you?" Sebastian tried again with the boy called Baxter. "You a boarder?"

"Yup, I'm bored all right," Baxter stated flatly (a pun Cheri would have appreciated). "Spent the whole afternoon. Watching Bristow here. Stuff his face."

"I have to maintain my blood sugar!" Bristow protested with a huff.

"You should be set for the next six months after today," Baxter deadpanned, then kept on talking before his friend could argue back. "Dude, listen." He turned his full attention to Sebastian, but his expression was unreadable behind his sunglasses. "Not to interrupt your one-eighties . . ."

"No worries," Sebastian said, his voice edged with hesitation.

"We just had to. Get out of. That plaza. Did you hear the mayor's speech?"

"Uh-huh." Sebastian nodded, the shock of black hair falling back into his eyes. Baxter, the short one, had a clipped way of speaking that made everything sound intense.

"Then you heard. That crazy stuff. About the supergirls?" Baxter asked.

"Yeah." Sebastian scuffed his sneaker against the bottom of his hoverboard.

"Totally crazy!" Bristow echoed. Apparently his bucket of chicken came with a smaller tub of mashed potatoes, which he was now shoveling into his mouth.

"Do you believe it?" the one named Baxter pressed. His pugnaciousness was making Sebastian uncomfortable. "That they're supergirls?"

Sebastian stalled. He'd been thinking all afternoon about Iris at that girl's birthday party, the way she'd put on such a light show. At the time he'd thought it was performance art. She'd *said* it was performance art. But now . . .

"Who knows, right?" he hedged, propping the board on its end and slowly spinning it around with dull slaps of his hand.

"We do," Baxter stated, matter-of-fact.

"We know all kinds of stuff about those girls," Bristow seconded, scraping the bottom of his mashed potato container with his plastic spoon.

Looking at the two other boys, Sebastian recalled finding them in the tree. He had been following a rainbow that ended there. *Iris's rainbow*, it dawned on him now. *She made it herself*. The realization somehow thrilled and upset him at the same time.

"Like what?" he asked, his throat catching.

Bristow and Baxter exchanged glances. Sebastian

thought he detected the shadow of a smile below the short kid's sunglasses.

"That intel is top secret." Bristow wiped his slick fingers on his blue satin sash. "Come with us and we'll fill you in. But you can't tell anyone."

"Intel?" Sebastian repeated, puzzled. Before he could ask for an explanation, he heard his own name, called out as a question.

"*Sebastian?*"

A tingle of recognition heated his ears, and the short hairs at the nape of his neck stood on end. He looked away from the river, past the two boys, up into the park. On the crest of a small hill, he could make out the silhouette. The sun was behind him now, but the girl seemed to be glowing all by herself. He couldn't quite see her face. But her curly purple hair was unmistakable.

Beside him on the promenade, Baxter followed his gaze. "You especially can't tell your *girlfriend*," he added when he spied the Ultra Violet. Above his black lenses one eyebrow arched up.

"I don't have a . . . She's not really my . . ." Sebastian stammered. What, exactly, did these two know about Iris? About him and Iris?

"So you guys weren't actually bird-watching that day here after all," he said softly, almost to himself. "You were . . . 'gathering intel'?"

At the memory of being trapped in the tree, Bristow turned red all over again. Sebastian didn't notice. His eyes were fixed on Iris on the hilltop.

She had stopped walking, as if she was hesitating, too. The silhouettes of her two friends soon appeared beside her. The short one with the ponytail grabbed her by the elbow, holding her back.

That seemed to animate Baxter for some reason, and his words took on more urgency. "Limited time offer, dude," he said, giving Bristow a nudge toward the exit. "Now or never."

Sebastian swallowed. He didn't know what to believe. Or whom to trust. There was more than something odd about these two boys. And yet . . . had Iris lied to him? About *everything?*

With a decisive flick of his wrist, Sebastian released his hoverboard. It dropped down into a horizontal position and floated at his feet. Tearing his eyes away from Iris, he stepped aboard. And skated after Bristow and Baxter, out of the park.

From the crest of the hill, the Ultra Violets watched, stunned. The frivolity of their little picnic was instantly forgotten. Iris felt as if a stone were stuck in her throat, and her eyes filled with tears. She breathed in shallow, shaky gasps, struggling to stop herself from blubbering like a baby. She'd tried so hard to juggle being a superhero and just being herself with Sebastian. But now it was all falling apart, like she'd always feared it would. He must have seen her performance at the plaza. She was sure he'd seen her on the hill. But he didn't answer back when she called his name. He didn't even wave good-bye.

Standing beside her, Scarlet was in just as much turmoil. She was not about to cry—Scarlet didn't do crying, not if she could help it. She did, however, have an overwhelming urge to run down the hill, run after the boys, and boot all three of them through the park gates like a bunch of soccer balls through goal posts. For the second time that afternoon, she clenched her hands into fists, her fingernails digging into the soft skin of her palms. She stomped the ground so hard that a bench on the orange brick promenade below popped out of its cement base.

Boys! she silently fumed. *I should have locked up that dirty spy Jack Baxter back at Opal's party when I had the chance!*

Cheri cradled Darth in her arms, looking from borderline-emotional-trainwreck Iris to seriously-in-need-of-anger-management Scarlet, and said what all three girls were thinking:

"OMV, RiRi. Did Sebastian just blow us off for the *Black Swans?*"

A Brand-New Bombshell

"IN A WORLD WHERE SUPERHEROES GO PUBLIC AND the boys they like blow them off..."

Iris did this thing during their lunch periods at Chronic Prep where she made up fake movies, imitating a voiceover in deep, dramatic tones while she recorded mini-films of the cafeteria on her smartphone. She'd started editing them on her tablet, adding title screens and special effects. She'd even created a channel for them on GoobToob, where the kids in their class could watch the videos and post comments.

But today Iris's smartphone lay on her cafeteria tray next to a grilled cheese sandwich gone cold. And Iris's voice was muffled and colorless, because her head was on the table, buried in her crossed arms.

Cheri and Scarlet looked at her, concerned. Even Darth dared to sneak out of his tote bag and skitter across the table to lift up a lock of Iris's hair and see if she was okay under all those ringlets. But still she didn't shift. She just sighed heavily. As her breath escaped, it blew up a few strands.

It hadn't been a bad day so far, their first back at school since they'd come out at Synchro de Mayo. Lots more kids came up to them, snapping pictures for their Smashface pages. Some eighth-grade girls on the cheerleading squad asked for Scarlet's help with a new routine. And a whole bunch of boys lined up at Cheri's locker bright and early in the morning to ask if she'd be their math tutor. Both girls just smiled—Cheri sweetly, Scarlet with a smirk—but didn't agree to anything. And if a kid (or a teacher) was especially pushy, the girls would refer them to Candace, who had set up a separate e-mail account for just these kinds of requests. The prescient teenius had anticipated this very phenomenon and warned them about it. "You girls have to save your energies for real emergencies," she'd said. "You can't just use your superpowers to be popular at school." Scarlet didn't care much about being popular, anyway—and definitely not with cheerleaders: She remained a bit suspicious of them after her run-ins with Opal's flunky, the two-faced BellaBritney. Cheri *did* care about her popularity. But she really had no interest in doing any more math for anyone.

Students had approached Iris that morning, too—or at least tried to. She seemed so distant, her periwinkle blue eyes staring off at nothing, that it was a bit intimidating. Those students who did risk venturing near found that, before they could actually reach her and open their mouths to speak, she disappeared. Vanishing right before their eyes. If they'd looked closely, they might have spotted a violet tendril here or there within the camouflage. But they were too freaked out and just turned and went the other way instead.

Now, at the lunch table, Cheri tried again to break through Iris's fugue.

"Are you sure you don't want to try texting him?" she suggested for the third time that day.

Iris shook her head no, her hair sweeping back and forth like a purple mop on the tabletop. "What if he doesn't answer? Then I'd just *die!* He HATES me now!" She let out a low moan.

"No way does he *hate* you," Cheri tried to reassure her, talking toward the crown of her head. She glanced over to Scarlet for support, but Scarlet just shook *her* head no and stayed mute. Cheri may have been the supermathematician of the group, but it was Scarlet who thought there was a fifty-fifty chance Sebastian *did* hate Iris—or at least was super miffed at her.

If some boy lied to me, Scarlet reasoned, *I'd be furious at him.* In fact, Agent Jack hadn't even lied about being a spy. He just WAS a spy. And *that* made her furious!

Struggling once again with her conflicted feelings for Jack—who, okay, had actually saved her life at Opal's party, dirty spy or not—Scarlet thumped the table. It clattered against the floor, sending Darth skidding back into the safety of his tote bag and finally rousing Iris.

Her eyes were all red from crying. Her face was all red from pressing it into her arms. Her hair was all in knots, like she'd just woken up. She stared out over their small table.

Past her cold grilled cheese sandwich. Beyond the cafeteria monitor and the huddle of jocks and Albert and the cool nerds. Until her red-rimmed baby blues met the equally doleful gaze of a brown-eyed girl.

Iris and Opal stared at each other across the cafeteria.

Scarlet and Cheri stared back and forth between them, nervous.

"Opal's sitting all alone," Cheri noted. Now that she was superpopular yet again, she could afford to feel a degree of sympathy for the ex-bestie who had uninvited her to her party.

Scarlet was unmoved. "Serves her right. She did try to brainwash the entire class!" she said, punching her thigh to keep from pounding the table again. "Owie," she muttered immediately afterward, massaging the sore spot.

"You said she cheered for me, right?" Iris asked listlessly, never once shifting her focus. "You said she complimented your dance?"

"Um, yes?" It was the truth, but Scarlet had the distinct feeling that, at this exact moment, the truth was the wrong answer.

"I'm going to go talk to her," Iris said.

"What?" Cheri exclaimed as Scarlet objected, "No!" Both girls started speaking at once, trying to persuade Iris against it.

"Maybe text her instead," Cheri said. "Even if you do get more bees with honey, that's a hornet's nest you don't want to poke in person, I don't think." She wasn't sure if those two expressions went together. Based on the scowl on Scarlet's face, she suspected no. "Plus, RiRi, you have a major case of bedhead, FYI," she whispered. "Not to upset you more, but I'd want you to tell me if *I* did."

"We shouldn't engage the enemy," Scarlet stated more directly. "Next thing you know, the whole cafeteria will be hit by a lightning storm, and then we'll *all* get detention!" Scarlet was on her longest non-detention streak ever, and she did not want to break it.

"Don't forget, she did try to electrocute you in the park," Cheri added, rummaging in her tote bag for her polka-dot umbrella just in case. "That afternoon after your date with—"

Darth popped up from the bag to wave his tail in front of Cheri's face before she could finish the sentence, but it was too late. The reminder of the date with Sebastian just depressed Iris more. And deepened her resolve.

"What else have I got to lose?" she said with a melodramatic toss of her tangles. She stood up from the table, ran a hand through her hair—which only made it messier, though Cheri didn't dare mention it twice—and strode across the cafeteria.

She sat down opposite Opal without asking, propped her chin in her hand, and stared some more, a pale ultraviolet aura humming around her. Opal began to blush a bit under the periwinkle spotlights, but she didn't blink. Every now and then, threads of amber ran through the brown of her eyes. Sensing the tension between the two girls, the other kids in the cafeteria began to skirt their chairs away from the epicenter of the encounter. But they still looked on, curious.

"Hi, Iris," Opal said at last, not sure if she should smile. "Your hair looks nice," she tacked on before she could help herself. From the day Iris returned to Sync City with her purple hair, Opal had hopelessly coveted it. She thought she'd be over it by now, but there it was again, the very first words out of her mouth.

"No, it doesn't," Iris said flatly back. She hadn't even bothered to wash it that morning, and Cheri had just told her it was basically a rat's nest of knots. "So don't lie right to my face."

"I'm not!" A spontaneous thunderclap punctuated Opal's protest, much to her chagrin. Whenever she and Iris got together, things always seemed to spin out of control.

"Then why are you being nice?" Iris challenged. "Scarlet told me she saw you in the crowd at Synchro de Mayo. She told me what you said."

Opal shifted in her seat, glancing around the rest of the cafeteria. Everyone was ogling them, but as she went to ogle back they all looked away—Albert Feinstein hurriedly returning to the game on his player; Julie Nichols whispering to Emma Appleby, who bobbed her head as she chewed her thumb; Brad Hochoquatro shooting his balled-up brown paper lunch bag into a trash can.

"I just . . ." Opal faltered.

"And where are your substitute besties?" Iris pressed on, too impatient to wait for Opal to answer. "Your O+2 crew?"

Opal tugged down the sleeves of her dress, her fingertips clutching the cuffs. "I'm not totally sure," she said. "After Karyn lost her tail, I think she got sent to some physical therapy place. And remember how I used to go to that all-girls' academy?"

Iris gave a reluctant nod. She didn't want to agree with Opal about anything, not even their history. But Opal had gone to an all-girls' academy at the same time that Iris was away at astronaut-offspring boarding school. After four years apart, the two had reunited at Chronic Prep. In that very cafeteria, in fact.

"Well, BellaBritney is going there now," Opal explained. "She said her parents hoped the discipline would teach her two selves to cooperate with each other."

Iris was silent. Now that they were actually talking, instead of blasting each other with sunrays and lightning bolts, she almost felt sorry for Opaline, too.

Maybe Opal sensed an opening, a hint of the girl who had tried more than once to patch up their friendship. Swallowing hard, she took a chance. "Anyway, those two were more like my, um, followers than my friends," she mumbled. "Not like how it was with you and . . . and the Ultra Violets."

Knock me over with a peacock feather, Iris thought. If Scarlet hadn't already warned her about their convo in the crowd, Iris might not have believed her ears. *Is Opal . . . eating mumble pie?!* She felt her mouth starting to smile. Until her brain reminded her heart how bummed out she was over Sebastian, and her lips set themselves straight again.

But Opal had seen that suggestion of a smile, and it was all the encouragement she needed. In a wavery voice, it all came spilling out.

"Iris, I know I've done some things, some *bad* things..."

"Like leading a mutant uprising?" Iris scoffed. "Or zombotomizing our entire class?" Mockery didn't come naturally to Iris. But she'd been zapped too many times by Opaline to let her guard down now. She slumped back in her chair, her arms folded across her chest. "Yeah, those were pretty bad all right!"

Opal grimaced. Not that she could blame Iris, but her sarcasm came as a bit of a shock: She was usually lollipop-sweet. Opal didn't expect this to be easy, though. And she couldn't stop now.

"I'm sorry," she confessed, as simply and sincerely as she could. Above just their table, it started to drizzle. Iris's ultraviolet heat evaporated the spritz before it could mist her, although the humidity still made her snarled hair double with frizz. Opal stayed dry, too—the rain she created, even unconsciously, respected her. But Iris thought she saw water in her eyes.

"Once you guys got superpowers," Opal said, "all of a sudden you were so sparkly, and Cheri was so brilliant, and Scarlet so graceful—it just wasn't fair! Because I was there that night in the FLab, too! And because ..."

Opal's voice broke, and the drizzle turned to droplets. As they splished against the tabletop, she paused, bowing her head and rubbing her temples. When she looked up again, the rain let up a little.

"And because I think I needed to feel powerful way more than any of you three," Opal continued in a deliberately calm tone. "Scarlet was brave to begin with. Cheri was already popular. You were confident and artistic. I wasn't any of those things—"

"Oh, Opal!" Iris blurted out, her heart softening. Opal held up a hand. Only so that she could keep talking while she still had the nerve. Iris did wince at the threat of a lightning strike, though.

"So when I finally grew them—grew superpowers—I guess it went to my head," Opal explained. "To have mutants, or the captain of the mathletes, at my command . . ." She trailed off, her gaze drifting over to Albert again. "Well, you know the rest," she said with a small shrug.

Iris stayed quiet this time, waiting to see if Opal was finished.

She wasn't.

"I miss you guys." Opal traced a finger through the puddle that had pooled on the tabletop. Tiny volts sparked off the water as she touched it. "Scarlet with her bad attitude, Cheri even when she's ditzy, and . . . and . . . I know you're mad at me, Iris, but you most of all. Will you take me back?"

It was a bombshell nearly as mind-blowing as the one BeauTek had made to package Opal's poison perfume. Iris's eyes widened in disbelief and her pupils shrank to dots, so that all Opal could see were two mesmerizing discs of violet-blue. Like a kaleidoscope, Iris's face flashed through umpteen different emotions in a riot of colors. Each pattern passed by so quickly, Opal couldn't focus on a single one. It was like watching a dream. The type of dream you don't understand at all when you're in it and, when you wake up from it, you can't remember a thing about. Just the sensation of it. That it was beautiful.

Then the bell rang. Without a word in response, Iris got up from the table, her skin drained of rainbow shades and pale once more. Opal watched her walk back to Cheri and Scarlet. Cheri gawked at Iris, questions in her eyes, while Scarlet glowered across the aisle at her.

Iris stood still for a moment, burying her hands in her mess of hair and blinking. She looked from Cheri, to Scarlet, and then over her shoulder to Opaline.

Suddenly a rush of emotions surged through her. As nuclear as a supernova, Iris burst into light. It shot out of her—her hands, her hair, her eyes, her mouth—burning into all four corners of the cafeteria. The other kids, even Scarlet and Cheri, cried out and cowered. If Iris had blazed for any longer than that infinitesimal Planck length, she would have blinded them all.

But it was only for a Planck unit. The briefest possible measurement of time. So *phew* no faces got melted.

Her temperature rapidly dropping again, Iris gasped "Oh!" at what she'd done. Brushing past her two besties, she bolted out of the cafeteria alone.

Never Say Never, Like, Ever
{*Roman Numeral 10 Is a Big, Fat Kiss!}

SO IRIS HAD A MOMENT. A SUPERNOVA DIVA MOMENT. Who *doesn't* every now and then? Anyone who doesn't, should. Because sometimes...

When the weight of the world is on your shoulders...

When it's (ugh) Monday...

When the boy you like gives you the cold shoulder before you ever make it to a second date...

When your once-upon-a-bestie asks you point-blank to take her back even though she has beyond betrayed you before...

And when, to top it all off, it's going to take an entire bottle of conditioner to undo all the gnots in your gnarly purple bedhead...

Then SOMETIMES you indulge your inner diva and storm out of a cafeteria all by yourself.

Given her artistic temperament, Iris was more prone to mood swings than the other Ultra Violets. Four years of astronaut-offspring boarding school and the influence of her highly logical scientist mother had done zero to squash her overflowing feelings. *Au contraire*, actually. Whenever Iris tried to gulp down her emotions, they had a way of gushing back up again at some even more awkward moment. Not that that excused being rude. Or going nuclear in the cafeteria. But she knew her friends would understand. Hopefully.

Being an artist, and therefore big on symbolic gestures, Iris had stopped by Tom's Diner on the way home from school to pick up some extra-special takeout. Then she took a soothing hot bubble bath—Darth hung out with her, soaking up the steam. After she'd wrapped her freshly washed hair in a clean towel, she texted Cher and Scar to come over ("please?") to CVUV for an emergency meeting. And while she waited for them to arrive, she fetched a carton of ice cream from the freezer.

When Cheri and Scarlet passed through the beaded curtain into the clubhouse, they were greeted by the sight of three slices of strawberry-rhubarb, each topped with a scoop of classic vanilla.

"Let me guess…" Cheri said, giggling.

Iris could feel the heat coloring her cheeks as she answered, "Yes, mumble pie. It's my turn to eat it."

"Yum!" Scarlet swooped in and scooped up a spoonful. "The rhubarb has a real kick!" she exclaimed—while literally kicking, of course.

"And the strawberry is *so sweet!*" Cheri teased. "Just like you, RiRi." She gave her friend a hug, which just made Iris blush more.

"You guys, I'm sorry I was such a diva at lunch today!" she apologized. "I'm sorry I solared out like that! The Sebastian thing has got me so bummed, and then Opal said some stuff that pushed me over the edge, I can't even!"

"We know," Scarlet said. She'd already finished her first piece of pie and was slicing a second. "We still love you, even when you're a radioactive drama queen!"

Iris was so relieved she thought she might start crying again. Luckily, she was pretty cried out from the weekend. "Thanks," she mumbled instead.

The girls settled into the clubhouse, Iris sitting sideways in the fuzzy orange egg chair, Cheri lounging across the marshmallow sofa with Darth in her lap, and Scarlet setting her second piece of strawberry-rhubarb beside the silver beanbag while she danced an impromptu lindy hop in front of the massive flower window.

"So, the suspense is making us dizzy!" she shouted, spinning to a stop. She flopped down into the beanbag and picked up her plate.

"Yes, do dish, Iris, *s'il vous plaît,*" Cheri said, feeding a strawberry to Darth. "What did Opal say?"

As she ran a wide-toothed comb through her wet hair, Iris repeated the conversation as best she could. She only verged toward emotional at the very end part—the part when Opal asked if the girls would take her back. The ice cream melting on her piece of mumble pie helped her keep a cool head.

"Whoa," Scarlet said when Iris had finished.

"OMV," Cheri agreed.

"I know!" Iris said.

"I mean, this is what we'd wanted for so long—for Opaline to come back…"

Frum da dark side! Darth thought, though only Cheri could hear him.

"But after everything she's done…" Scarlet shook her ponytail. "Cher, didn't you say there was only, like, a one-in-gazillion chance Opal would ever turn good again?"

"Not *exactly*," Cheri demurred. As her mind raced to find a formula in which her hopes were equal to or greater than the statistical data, her hair took on its magenta pink tint. "I think I said the likelihood was that she would go badder first. Which she did! With the whole poison perfume thing! So maybe she's peaked—like on a chronological line graph. And now her rate of meanness is in decline?"

The green of Cheri's eyes blinked with a chart that hypothetically tracked the downward progression of Opal's evildoing.

Iris and Scarlet didn't even bother exchanging confused glances. By now they'd gotten used to Cheri peppering her comments with mathematical terms. Terms that were kind of like the diametric opposite (see? That was one of them right there!) of her funny slips of tongue. "Mumble pie" made Iris and Scarlet laugh. "Chronological line graph" made them think. Most of the time, if they just paid attention to the rest of what Cheri was saying, they figured out her meaning. Eventually.

Iris was working on an especially snaggly knot. From behind her scrim of wet ringlets she said, "I just remember how she told me she'd 'never ever ever'—like, ever!—get back together with us. Though that was before her birthday party disaster."

"Never say never?" Scarlet offered. "Isn't that what the song says?"

Each girl sat with her thoughts for a minute. Well, Scarlet didn't sit with hers—she danced a bolero, trying to remember the rest of the lyrics to that never song. With each sharp turn she made, she considered a new side to the controversial topic of Opal's return. Cheri had taken out her sequined lilac nail polish again and was touching up her manicure as she talked things over with Darth: Since Opal had tried to take the superpowered skunk from the Ultra Violets, his vote definitely counted. And Iris, tucking her damp strands behind her ears, tapped open her tablet computer to draft one of her helpful pros-and-cons lists. She wrote it down with her rhinestone stylus:

COOLNESS?

1. Opaline is our best friend from all the way back in kindergarten.
2. She was with us in the FLab when we got slimed by the goo, so she is an Ultra Violet, too.
3. We took a BFF vow and sealed it with wax!
4. It is totally understandable how she lost it when she saw Albert kissing Cheri. (Now that Iris was having romantic turmoil of her own, she felt a newfound sympathy for Opal on this particular point.)
5. Her powers could maybe help us fight mutants.
6. She has insider knowledge of BeauTek.
7. Everyone makes mistakes.
8. Everyone deserves a second chance.

LAMENESS!

1. Opaline led a mutant uprising.
2. She started that prune-juice rumor about me!
3. She tried to take Darth from Cheri!!
4. She shot lightning bolts at Scarlet during her school play audition!!!
5. And almost electrocuted me in Chrysalis Park!!!!
6. And zombotomized most of our class at her birthday party (! x 5)
7. Where she also tried to bowl me over with high-voltage balls (! x infinity)
8. Fool us once, shame on you; fool us twice, shame on us?

Cheri came over from the sofa, Darth riding on her shoulder. Scarlet finished her bolero with a definitive foot stomp, then hooked her arms over the back of the fuzzy egg chair. Iris held up her tablet so that both girls could see the list she'd written.

"A tie," Cheri said, noting how the pros and cons lined up.

"I can't decide, either," Scarlet said as she scanned the two columns. "The bottom line is, after everything that's happened, I just don't know if I can ever *trust* Opal again."

Iris sighed. She always wanted to believe the best of people. Believe they could change for the better. But Opal had really hurt her, inside and out! Iris couldn't help it: She felt the same as Scarlet did.

But more than just their friendships was at stake.

"I hate to be so calculating—" Iris began.

"Hey, that's usually my jam!" Cheri interrupted. "Calculating, multiplying, dividing . . ." She and Darth high-fived at the joke.

"Seriously," Iris said with a smile, "our personal feelings aside, we've got to think strategically about this, too. How can we find out what Develon Louder and Mayor Blumesberry were talking about? And Cher, you were right to bring up the poison perfume yesterday. How can we be sure it's all been destroyed?"

Cheri read down the *Coolness?* column again, her eyes lingering on the points about mutants and BeauTek. "Hmm, that does add up, RiRi. Even if we don't trust Opal, it could help to have her on our side."

Scarlet did a backward cartwheel. "Like, keep your friends close," she said, landing in a split on the shag rug, "and your frenemies closer."

We Interrupt This Gym Class . . .

PSHREEEEEEEEEET!

The shrill peal of Ms. Skynyrd's platinum whistle brought the girls in Chronic Prep's gymporium to a halt. Scarlet had just dropped to her knees and bumped the volleyball four inches (Cheri did this calculation) before it hit the floor. It arced up over the net, bonking first a distracted Lillian, then a giggling Gillian Jensen on their identical twin heads before bouncing out of bounds and underneath the bleachers.

Darth, who was hiding there in Cheri's bag, watched it roll by.

"Owie," the sisters whined together, each rubbing the sore spot on the other one's head.

Scarlet straightened up. "That was a clean shot," she said loud enough for Ms. Skynyrd to hear, wondering why the teacher had stopped the game. "No foul play." She glanced across the net at her opponents.

Opaline had ended up on the other team, which was

just as well. The Ultra Violets were still unsure what to do about her. Since the start of school that morning, they'd been friendly—but from a distance. The way you might be with cousins you only see on holidays. Her other classmates were being even less nice—understandably, considering her recent attempt to turn them into zombos.

"Bleachers, girls!" Ms. Skynyrd commanded with a clap of her hands, completely ignoring Scarlet's commentary. The gym teacher shoved up the sleeves of her black-and-yellow tracksuit, then gripped one of the volleyball poles and began turning it toward the other until the net resembled a giant, tightly wound scroll.

Evidently, PE was ending early today.

Breaking off into their usual cliques, all the girls took to the bleachers. Rachel Wright snapped the elastic at the end of her braid back in place. Abby O'Adams snapped her gum. Emma Appleby tugged at her shorts, which were a little too, um, that.

"Cheeky," Iris joked as she started up the benches.

"Did Emma get taller, too?" Scarlet muttered, cutting a sidelong glance at the classmate who had outgrown her uniform. As far as Scarlet could tell, other girls were always getting taller, just not her.

"Maybe?" Cheri replied as she casually retrieved her tote bag—and their mascot. "I'm not really sure." She actually thought Emma might have gotten a bit *wider* . . .

But dont sez dat! Darth thought, peeking his head out to see for himself.

Oh, I'd never! Cheri answered. *That would not be nice.*

The three Ultra Violets sat down on the top row of the bleachers, their backs against the wall. From the bottom bench, Opal cast a forlorn look their way, blinking her brown eyes at them like an abandoned puppy dog. Iris pretended not to notice, occupying herself with a brand-new knot in her hair. Cheri offered a mild smile before turning her attention to her suddenly fascinating manicure. Scarlet's immediate reaction was to wrinkle her nose and raise her fist. Opal twisted back around the minute she saw that.

"Oops," Scarlet said, switching to a small hand wave when it was already too late. "Old habits die hard."

It was only then that the girls noticed the ginormous video monitor descending from a slot in the ceiling. Its molded corners brushed against the climbing ropes as it lowered down. All the classrooms in Chronic Prep had similar monitors, but the one in the gymporium, like the one in the auditorium, was jumbo-sized. It came to a stop just above the basketball net, which swung beneath it like scraggly white whiskers.

"A citywide announcement," Iris said, giving up on the hair knot as Ms. Skynyrd trotted over to join the students. "This must be important." The teacher sat next to Opal.

A sharp buzz of static crackled through the speakers,

amplified by the gymporium's fiberglass walls. Girls rushed to cover their ears as the screen blipped to life, thousands of bitmapped Technicolor rectangles gradually resolving into a single image. Beaming down at them in high-definition 3-D, her ruddy face some ten feet square, was Mayor Rosenmary Blumesberry. A silver banner emblazoned with the seal of SynchroniCity hung from her podium.

Darth let out a little squeak at the sight and burrowed back into his bag.

"But she can't see us, right?" Scarlet asked, slouching down in her seat.

"I don't think so," Iris said. "I mean, cameras must be everywhere"—she scanned the gym, realizing she'd never really thought much about it before—"but wouldn't it be hard for the mayor to speak if she was watching video images of everyone in the entire city all at the same time?"

"It's creepy," Scarlet stated plainly. "And not in a good horror-movie way. I wish we were still playing volleyball." All around them, their classmates were having some version of the same conversation. All except Opal, who sat mute beside Ms. Skynyrd. The teacher was gesturing for the girls to quiet down.

"SHUSH!" suddenly boomed throughout the gymporium, stunning everyone into silence. Ms. Skynyrd slapped a hand across her mouth as if, for an instant, she thought *she* was the one who'd shouted it. Until she searched across the gym and spotted her bullhorn all the way on the other side. The order had been much too loud.

On-screen, the gale-force wind of the colossal shush had flipped up half of Mayor Blumesberry's root-beer-brown hair like she'd been blasted sideways by a blow-dryer. A pair of hands came into view, briskly combing the layers back into place.

"I bet those hands belong to her personal stylist," Cheri confided. "Can you imagine it's somebody's job just to follow the mayor around, freshening up her makeup and fixing her hair all day long?"

"That could be useful." Iris frowned at her vexsome violet knot again. The curls must have gotten tangled during the volleyball game. Iris wondered, and not for the first time, if her hair had a mind of its own.

Camera-ready once more, Mayor Blumesberry began to speak.

"Citizens of Sync City," she said, a big smile on her face. "After the joyous celebration of Synchro de Mayo this past weekend, I'm breaking into your Tuesday to bring you this special announcement about our newest initiative—"

"BEAUTEKIFY!" The shout came from offscreen, flattening half of the mayor's hair again. Just as the disembodied hands of the stylist re-entered the frame, the screen froze.

All the girls stared at the stalled image of a bitmapped Mayor Blumesberry, her hair vertically shocked, her eyebrows peaked in surprise, her mouth caught in an *Oh!* The thin teeth of the stylist's comb sawed out in 3-D over the bleachers. In the center of the screen, dots blinked in a circle, indicating that the live stream was rebuffering.

Then the transmission kicked in again, and all the digital tiles of the still image rapidly dissolved to a live shot of the mayor blotting the shine from her cheeks with dabs of her giant powderpuff. Caught in the act, she personally froze in this new pose for another split second before the random stylist hands appeared once more to take the powderpuff away. Or try to. The mayor refused to let go, and a dusty tug-of-war took place on-screen until the stylist gave up.

"As I was saying"—the mayor fanned a hand through the air to dispel the cloud of powder—"on behalf of the city council, and with the generous sponsorship of the BeauTek Corporation, I'm proud to announce, effective immediately, Projekt BeauTekification."

"This had better not be some lame reality show…" Scarlet muttered.

"Whatever it is, it can't be good," Iris hissed back.

"Not if BeauTek's behind it," Cheri seconded.

Oh swell no, Darth thirded the thought.

"Starting, hmm, about a couple of days ago now," the mayor said, "BeauTek, er, *volunteers* will be in Chrysalis Park. Shampooing the trees. Waxing the grass to keep it neat and trim. Glamming up the squirrels with blue eye shadow…"

I piteez da fool who try dat! Dart snickered from his hiding place in Cheri's tote bag.

"Sync City is a grand metropolis," Mayor Blumesberry continued, "with its glass and steel towers, its formerly modern monorail, its aeroscootering commuters. How can nature be expected to compete without some cosmetic help?"

"IT CAN'T!" The bellowing came again from off-camera. This time the mayor must have anticipated it, because she ducked down behind her podium before the blast could mess up her hair once more. The Sync City banner flapped out in 3-D over the bleachers.

When Mayor Blumesberry popped back up, her smile appeared slightly strained, and beneath the cakey layer of white powder her cheeks flushed russet with embarrassment. But she carried on with her announcement. "No, no, it can't," she responded to the camera, as if the citizens had asked her the question and not the other way around. "That's what Projekt BeauTekification is all about: natural beauty—only better!"

"GRASS SKIRTS!"

Although not wearing one herself, Mayor Blumesberry swayed to this latest shout in an accidental hula dance. "And you'll recognize the volunteers by their cheerful grass skirts!" she explained, regaining her composure.

A photo inset showed a beaming worker in a grass skirt the same acidic yellow as the Mall of No Returns's neon sign.

The same bilious chartreuse as its shopping bags—the ones Opal's mom had used to pack the poisonous perfume at her daughter's birthday disaster. Iris, being an artist, searched for the good in all colors. But something about that sharp sulfuric yellow made her eyes hurt.

"I saw some weird tourists wearing those at Synchro de Mayo!" Cheri gasped, just as the image vanished from the screen.

"So if you pass someone in a sassy grass skirt dabbing perfume behind a pigeon's ears or brushing a beaver's front teeth or, *ahem-tee-hee-ha*, powdering the harbor," the mayor concluded in a rush, "stop and take a moment to say thank you. Thank you for making Sync City more pretty!"

The picture froze again, Mayor Blumesberry's giant 3-D grin looming over the girls in the gymporium as if she would snap all their heads off in a single bite. Scarlet didn't think she could slouch any lower on the bleachers, but she did. Sometimes being small had its advantages.

"That is the dumbest waste of money I ever heard of," she said from her spot next to Iris's feet.

Darth chittered something to Cheri.

"I know!" she exclaimed. "Chrysalis Park is perfect as it is. Putting makeup on squirrels is totally pointless. Plus, almost nobody can pull off blue eye shadow, alas."

With a whir that echoed throughout the gymporium, the supersized monitor began its ascent back into its storage slot, the ceiling swallowing up the mayor's fixed grimace. Girls began to make their way down the stands and toward the locker room. As Iris reached the exit doors, she turned to face Scarlet and Cheri.

"Obvi that was Develon shouting in the background," she said. "This Projekt BeauTekification must be what she was talking to the mayor about."

Over her friends' shoulders, Iris could see Opaline, still in the middle of the gym. She was helping Ms. Skynyrd tidy up, slowly, though there really wasn't much to be put away before the next period. Iris suspected she must have been stalling to avoid the crowd in the locker room. Again, she couldn't stop from feeling a little sorry for her. And again, her *Coolness?/ Lameness!* list ran through her mind.

Iris yanked anxiously on the stubborn knot in her hair as Scarlet and Cheri looked back at Opal, too. "I'm going to text Candace," she said, continuing through the exit. "She'll know how to break the tie."

At the mayor's office, as soon as the cameras had been shut off, Rosenmary Blumesberry undid the top button of her blouse and ran her jacket sleeve across her sweaty forehead. A smear of white powder soiled the dark fabric.

"How was that?" she said in the direction of the broadcast's invisible bloviator.

Develon Louder, president of BeauTek, stepped out

from behind the scenes. A bottle of bubbly in one hand, two long-stemmed glasses in the other, and her black Burkant handbag hanging from the crook of her arm, she approached the mayor with complete confidence—despite the fact that she was teetering on six-inch heels. Once she reached Mayor Blumesberry—who would have been a good deal shorter than her even if she hadn't been wearing stilettos—she popped off the cork with an assured jerk of her thumb. It shot up to the rafters as frothy bubbles spewed out of the bottle's mouth. Placing the flutes on the podium, she filled each one high enough for foam to spill over their thin lips, too. Then she put the bottle down, picked a glass up, and swung around her pocketbook until it was directly in front of her face.

Through a thin transparent panel that ran around its top, she peered down at the mayor.

"LEGENDARY, BLUMESBERRY!" she barked, just as she'd been barking all throughout the broadcast. "Projekt Beau*Toxification* is underway!" From behind her black Burkant, she took a celebratory sip, then pointed to the second flute with a sharply filed fingernail.

"Thanks," the mayor said, raising her glass in a toast. "Don't mind if I do."

Second Helpings

YOU WOULD THINK THAT, AFTER PARTY-CRASHING Opal's birthday and basically blowing up the back room in a single awesome solar event, the Ultra Violets would never want to set foot inside Tom's Diner again. Too many bad memories. Too mucho bad mojo. But that would be crazy talk! The Ultra Violets don't get all superstitious about stuff like that! (Well, maybe Candace does, a little bit, sometimes. Which is utterly baffling considering she's just a few college credits short of becoming an official scientist and thus should be the most rational of the bunch.) It wasn't the diner's fault that it had been the site of a bombastic superhero showdown. And Tom's Diner had the best berry parfaits and butterbeer and curly fries in Sync City. AND the girls had grown quite fond of their sassy unflappable beehived waitress—a woman who had seen it all but didn't seem to care about any of it.

The sassy waitress was so unflappable, in fact, that when the three Ultra Violets cruised down on their robotic hummingbird wings and entered the diner after school on Tuesday, she barely blinked at their now public superhero status. She just called, "Yo, Philippe!" across the dining room, then slapped her hip with her notepad.

And just like that, the girls' favorite table opened up.

"Is that a velvet rope?" Cheri cooed as the busboy unlatched it in front of the booth. He gave the red vinyl bench a final towel-buffing before stepping aside and gallantly bowing while she slipped in and sat down. He was a rather crush-worthy busboy, Cheri couldn't help but notice, with neatly parted ash-blond hair and a prominent curve to the cupid's bow of his lips.

"*Merci, Philippe*," she said with her sparkliest smile.

"*C'est mon plaisir, mademoiselle*," he answered in perfect French, his gray-gold eyes twinkling right back at her.

"Did you hear that?" Cheri gushed to the other two girls as he headed off to clean another table. "He said it was his pleasure!"

"Oh brother!" Scarlet gave Cher an eye roll. She may not have been superstitious like Candace, but Scarlet definitely was suspicious of flowery sweet talk, especially in a foreign language. *Jack would never say something all stupid and gooey like that*, she found herself thinking. Instantly annoyed that she'd stopped being mad at the Black Swan even for a minute, Scarlet gave her head an aggressive shake. As if she could knock the lil' agent out of it. As if!

"Are you all right?" Iris asked, sliding into the booth beside her.

"I just don't have time for boys, okay?" Scarlet said vehemently. "We have more important things to worry about!"

"I'm sorry!" Iris exclaimed, her face breaking out in purple paisleys. "I've tried not to obsess any more about Sebastian, at least not out loud, I—"

"No, no, no!" Scarlet shook her head again, loosening her ponytail elastic until her licorice-black hair tumbled out of it. "I didn't mean that. I didn't mean you. I . . . Oh, never mind. Hey, check this out!" she said, spotting a welcome distraction. A small brass plaque had been added beneath the window. Scarlet read the engraved words:

TOM'S DINER
Designated Booth of the
ULTRA VIOLETS:
Saviors of Sync City,
Connoisseurs of
Milkshakes

"Our own VIP booth!" Cheri beamed. "Awesome!"

"What does 'connoisseurs' mean?" Scarlet asked.

"Like, experts," Iris said, smiling. "We're milkshake experts!"

"That's a French word, too," Cheri added, a dreamy look in her emerald-green eyes. "Maybe Philippe wrote it. Maybe this VIP booth was his idea . . ."

"Oh. Brother!" Scarlet objected again, twisting her hair back up into its ponytail.

Just then, Candace pushed through the diner's doors. Seeing the girls in their usual booth, she gave a wave and headed over to join them.

"Sorry I'm late, guys," she explained, sitting down next to Cheri. "The cumulus were pretty thick coming from the FLab, and it took me a while to remotely park the cloudship." She flashed the screen of her smartphone, but all the girls could see was a field of fluffy white. Their prism-covered aircraft was impossible to detect within it.

The sassy waitress sashayed over to the table, notepad at the ready. She must have been running low on hairspray, because her black-and-white-striped updo was collapsing in the middle, making it look more like a big bird's nest than a beehive. Philippe had also circled back around and was now clearing plates off the table directly behind theirs.

"The usual, ladies?" the waitress asked with a crack of her chewing gum, not bothering with any effusive "OMV you three are superheroes" small talk.

"We're going to try something different today!" Iris responded, while Cheri and Scarlet nodded along. With their newfound appreciation of pie, humbly, mumbly, tart, or sweet, they'd decided to taste every type on the menu at least once. Also, ordering pie greatly decreased the chances of Candace accidentally pilfering another swizzle spork, since those mostly came with parfaits. "A piece of blueberry cobbler for me," Iris said.

"Straight up coconut cream," Scarlet ordered.

"And I'd like—" Cheri began.

Azk her, pleez! From his hiding spot in her bag, Darth nudged Cheri's leg with his nose.

Cheri pursed her lips, but she found it impossible to deny Darth anything, even when she already knew the answer—and when a cute busboy was eavesdropping on their order. Clearing her throat, she said, "You wouldn't happen to have a slice of grub-earthworm pie, would you?" She was too embarrassed to meet the sassy waitress's skeptical eyes.

"Sorry, hon, all sold out," the waitress replied without missing a beat. "That was yesterday's special."

Darn! Darth thought.

I'm sure she's being sarcastic! Cheri thought back as she smiled sheepishly at the waitress. "Then just cherry for me."

"How 'bout you, Moms?"

By now Candace was certain the waitress had to know that no way was she the girls' mom. But she'd given up trying to correct her. "Key lime, please," was all she said.

As the waitress strutted away, Candace leaned in to the center of the table and looked out over her geek-chic glasses. "Okay, first things first. What's the gut check on Projekt BeauTekification?"

All four of them placed great value on the gut check. The

gut check was not to be confused with superstition. The gut check was all about knowing how to trust your intuition—the undefinable, pit-of-your-stomach feeling that something was either right or wrong.

"You saw the broadcast today, too?" Cheri asked.

"It was impossible to miss," Candace answered. "Mayor Blumesberry overrode all the networks in Sync City. It came up on the main screen in the FLab. She must have a pretty powerful computer server to do that. Of course, I operate all of *our* tech—our cell phones and tablets, the robo-wings, the MAUVe, the cloudship, and all the equipment in Club Very UV—off my own private satellite, so we didn't get hacked. It's one thing for the Ultra Violets to publicly serve Sync City, but I'm not down with the mayor having access to everyone's TVs and computers. Especially not ours. Not if she's in cahoots with BeauTek!"

"Something's totally unkosher about it," Scarlet agreed, just as the waitress arrived with their order.

"Purple sings the blues," she announced, serving Iris her cobbler. "Cherry for Red, hold the worms," she joked to Cheri. "Lime time for Moms. And for the peanut, coconut cream!" With a flourish, she placed the last plate in front of Scarlet.

Scarlet forced a smile. "Thanks," she mumbled through her first mouthful of pie. The waitress seemed to take a special delight in teasing her, and there wasn't much Scarlet could do besides grin and deal.

At the tartness of the lime, Candace puckered up. "We need to get to the bottom of the Projekt," she said through pinched lips as the waitress shuffled away on her orthopedic sneakers. "Find out what it's really about. Maybe I can counter-hack the mayor's systems. And figure out the best way to infiltrate BeauTek." She went to drum her fingers on the tabletop thoughtfully, but ran them into her pie mousse instead.

"That brings us to the second thing second," Iris said, plucking a few napkins from the tabletop dispenser and passing them to Candace.

"You mean Opaline?" Candace replied, sucking cool green cream off her thumb.

"How did you know?" Iris sat up straight with surprise. "She said she wants to join the Ultra Violets!"

"Wow, really?" Candace's eyebrows rose to meet the ends of her baby bangs. "That is a newsflash!" She began poking around in her bag for her bottle of all-purpose decontaminant. Teenius scientists packed decontaminant at all times.

"Yup," Scarlet said, licking her spoon clean. "Girlfriend ate the mumble pie."

Cheri frowned. "That's just what I called it by accident," she explained to Candace, embarrassed again. After the humiliation of attempting to order an earthworm delicacy for their clandestine skunk mascot, she really did not want to relive another one of her verbal blunders. "What Scarlet means is, Opal said she was sorry. To Iris."

"Wait, Candace, so if you didn't know about that, then what did you think we meant?" Iris wondered.

"That her mom left BeauTek," Candace stated bluntly, "and she's back at the FLab."

"What?!" all three girls cried out together, their voices overlapping as they said things like, "How is that even possible?" and "Doing what?" and "Who hired her?" and "Don't our moms know about BeauTek?"

While the girls got all their questions out in the open, Candace pushed down on the pump of the decontaminant container. A squirt of gelatinous liquid shot right up onto her eyeglasses. "I don't know all the details yet," she said, taking them off before the gel dripped onto her dessert. "But I believe she went through an intensive interview process, and then she had to be deprogrammed, and she's employed on a temporary basis only. Like a trial run."

"But without Dr. Trudeau, we don't have an inside track to BeauTek!" Iris despaired, slumping back against the padded vinyl booth. "That's how I thought we might infiltrate it. Through Opaline and her mother!"

Hands and glasses sanitized and spotless once more, Candace put away the decontaminant and picked up her plain old, completely boring, non-swizzly spoon. Savoring another taste of her key lime pie, she eyed Scarlet, who by then was balancing her own spoon on the tip of her nose. "Don't you girls—you in particular, Scar—have another connection to BeauTek?" Candace floated the question.

Scarlet twitched her nose, and the spoon clanged onto the table. "Meaning what?" she demanded.

"The Black Swans!" Cheri's eyes fluttered wide. "I daresay Agent Jack is sweet on you, Miss Scarlet Jones," she teased. "Maybe you could infiltrate his heart!"

"I daresay shut up!" Scarlet retorted, kicking the table. Iris and Cheri burst into giggles.

"Girls, calm down!" Candace implored, wishing she had a spork to brandish. "Seriously, the Black Swans could be the way to go. A way to kill two birds—"

Seeing Cheri's suddenly stricken expression, Candace quickly changed hers. "A way to *do two things at once*," she substituted. "Find out about Projekt BeauTekification and test Opaline."

"You mean get Opaline to investigate the Black Swans as a way for her to prove her loyalty?" Scarlet asked, secretly relieved that it wouldn't force her into another confrontation with Agent Jack.

"As long as it doesn't involve killing birds!" Cheri said as she fed Darth a jam-coated cherry. He squeezed his eyes shut at the sweetness. *Tell me that isn't better than some gross grub!* Cheri chided.

Iz an akqwired tayst, Darth shrugged, holding out his paws for more fruity goodness.

"We're all just so afraid to trust Opal again," Iris summed up for the three of them.

"I'd be worried, too," Candace said. "But this could be what we've hoped for from the beginning, guys. The *four* original Ultra Violets, together at last!"

Iris, Scarlet, and Cheri each glanced around the booth, remembering the time they'd been there with Opal after the ballet. Before everything went wrong.

"Everyone deserves a second chance, right?" Candace prompted. "Especially old friends."

Iris twirled one of her violet ringlets thoughtfully. "That was the last point on my *Coolness?* list," she said. "Giving Opal a second chance."

"Did somebody say 'seconds'?" The sassy waitress must

have had pretty sharp hearing. She approached the table again and clicked her pen. "You cuckoo for more coconut, Short Stuff?" she asked Scarlet. "Who here gets a second helping?"

Iris took a deep breath, then raised her pinkie finger in a mini-salute of sorts. "Opal does, I guess."

The Makeup Test

OPAL GOT IT. NO, SHE DID. SHE'D DONE SOME PRETTY bad things. Some *crazy* bad things. The Ultra Violets would have to be crazy themselves to just take her back with open arms, no questions asked, unconditionally. It made 100 percent sense for them to put her to a test first. To prove her loyalty. Opal understood that. No, she did.

But that didn't mean it didn't make her feel small and ashamed and a little bit sick.

It was Iris who'd come to her with the proposal, during recess on Wednesday. Since it was Iris she'd asked to take her back, that made 100 percent sense, too. But did Cher and Scar hate her so much that they couldn't even stand talking to her? Opal could still hear Scarlet's threat from Synchro de Mayo—*"I'm watching you!"*—ringing in her ears. She could still see her raised fist in gym class.

"Oh, not at all!" Iris had tried to downplay their absence. "They both just had a, um, a scheduling conflict! Scarlet is in the auditorium with Ms. von Smith, choreographing a routine she wants to perform at the Gazebra. And Mr. Grates asked Cheri to tutor an exchange student who's having trouble with exponents. That's why they're not here."

Iris had nodded a bit too eagerly, Opal thought. Giving her a dubious look, she'd replied, "Okay"—what else could she say?—before asking, "So what is it you want me to do?"

The more Opal brooded about it now, the darker charcoal-gray the clouds turned overhead. All except one, she noticed, which stayed surprisingly pale.

"Looks like rain!" Albert observed.

"Looks like." Opal managed a wan smile. Striking an uneasy deal with the Ultra Violets was one thing. Making up with Albert Feinstein was a whole other kettle of Swedish Fish. Opal was still bewildered by how *that* had happened. Maybe she was on a spontaneous apology tour and once she got started she couldn't stop? One minute she was answering a question in math about negative numbers; the next, Albert was blathering at her locker about how negative numbers were "assigned to black's position in online chess" (um, okay . . .); and that just reminded her again of how he'd asked her on a chess date but she'd smoked his note with a lightning bolt. All of a sudden she was mumbling something about how she hadn't really meant to briefly hijack his brain just before her birthday (even though at the time she really had) and . . .

And he'd laughed it off. He hadn't even seemed that mad!

Nervous, maybe, nerdy for sure, but not mad. He just made some weird, vague comment about how it wasn't his brain she'd hijacked but "another vital organ." What did *that* mean?

"No," Opal had stammered, trying to stick to the facts. "It was definitely your brain!" And then, because talking to Albert was so unbearably awkward and other kids walking by in the hallway were giving them funny looks and snickering and whispering and she was worried she might lose control and go electrical, she put an end to the whole embarrassing encounter by asking him to join her on this outing—not mentioning, of course, the minor detail that she'd be on a mission for the Ultra Violets.

He'd said yes immediately. She'd immediately regretted it, slamming her locker shut and rushing off to her next class. But now there they were. Sitting at one of the outdoor chess tables behind the Gazebra by the riverside. The black-and-white squares of the gameboard matched the black-and-white stripes of the pavilion.

A strangely familiar scent tickled Opal's nose, and she turned her head to sneeze into her shoulder.

"Gesundheit!" Albert declared with a geeky gusto that didn't quite vibe with his cool haircut and clothes. "Pollen counts are at record highs this season."

"Are they?" Opal echoed, distracted by the smell. It didn't help her mindset knowing that Iris, Cheri, and Scarlet were somewhere nearby—"an undisclosed location" was all Iris would say—listening in on every word. Opal berated herself again for asking Albert along. Blinking across the chessboard in response to his curious glance, she couldn't decide if the combo of his dorky interior and trendy exterior was interesting or annoying. Real or fake.

Then again, she mused, *I'm not sure what's real or fake about me these days, either.*

The best she could do, she figured, was stay calm and not shock anyone. Not only would that be bad, but it would probably also fry the wireless microphone Candace had embedded in her barrette.

Albert went to move his white knight on the chessboard. He was winning the game easily. Opal wasn't forfeiting on purpose, she just had a test to pass. She pretended to contemplate her next move, fingering one of her black pawns.

But really she was awaiting the arrival of the Black Swans.

I guess I'm a pawn, too, she thought, *in this weird spy game.*

Opal had known that her mother, the esteemed if high-strung Dr. Trudeau, scientist-slash-publicist extraordinaire, had signed two boys to an espionage contract back before she'd left BeauTek. But it was only when Iris had shown her satellite images that Opal realized she'd already met them.

"Agent Sidney Bristow," she'd read off the e-file in the schoolyard. The obnoxious boy with the hot dog breath. "And Agent Jack Baxter." The boy with the salt-and-pepper hair who'd pulled him away.

"Even though we know their names now, we call them Big Red and Lil' Freckles. It bugs them." Iris's expression had been serious, but there was a twinkle of mischief in her pale blue eyes. "Scarlet won't admit it, but the short one totally likes her," she'd confessed.

Opal had nodded then, keeping her expression serious, too—not risking a giggle or a smirk. It was information Iris didn't have to share—maybe she didn't even mean to, maybe it just slipped out by accident. Opal held it close anyway, because it was the kind of secret one friend would tell another. So it made her feel like maybe, just maybe, she and Iris were becoming friends again. Scarlet had always been such a tough tomboy: The thought of an actual boy crushing on her . . . somehow it was sort of hilarious. That said boy was a spy for BeauTek would have been even more hilarious if it wasn't so dangerous.

"And why are they the Black Swans?" Opal had asked Iris that afternoon in the schoolyard. "What's that code for?"

"Well, it's complicated." Iris had tugged on one of her lovely purple ringlets, thinking. "But basically it has to do with a theory about unpredictable phenomena. And because they always wear black suits."

"I met them," Opal had shared back as she scanned the biographical data on Iris's tablet. "In civilian clothes. The big one came up to me in the crowd at Synchro de Mayo, he asked me if I . . ." Opal had paused. Heat rushed to her cheeks, and suddenly her Peter Pan collar felt terribly tight around her throat, but she swallowed hard and looked Iris in the eye. "He asked me if I knew any mutants."

Iris had recoiled then, taking a quick step back. Opal knew she was remembering the mutant battle in BeauTek's Vi-Shush lab. But she held Opal's gaze, too. "What did you tell him?" she asked coolly.

"I didn't. I didn't say anything, Iris, I swear. I just made a joke about how maybe *he* was a mutant."

At that, Iris appeared to relax a little. Then her eyes lit up. "I bet that's why they scoped you out at Synchro de Mayo!" she said with a snap of her fingers that set off little ultraviolet sparks. "They must know something about the mutants! And they already know who your mom is. Do they know that she left BeauTek?"

"Maybe not . . ." Opal had realized. "Maybe they think that she's still on BeauTek's side."

"Meaning they think you are, too."

"On Team BeauTek?"

"It's perfect for our plan"—Iris had given her an intense look then, so intense Opal could feel the rays blazing from her eyes—"but you'd just better not be in real life!"

Across the chess table from her, Albert cleared his throat, breaking into her thoughts. "By my calculations, you have thirteen potential courses of action," he analyzed, "all of which, ultimately, will still result in my checkmating your king."

Opal left her pawn where it was and looked up from the chessboard, expecting Albert to be grinning at her in full-on nerd triumph. But no, his smile was hesitant. "You wouldn't want me to lose on purpose, would you?" he asked. The way he said it, it sounded like he was sorry he hadn't.

Opal's stomach did a small flip-flop. Behind Albert's trendy façade, there was still the dweeby mathlete. But behind both of those personas, maybe Albert was sincerely sweet. Maybe that was why she was drawn to him even before his makeover. A rush of affection ran through her. Impulsively, she reached across the table and gave him a playful poke in the chest. It crackled with static electricity where she touched him. "Lose on purpose?" she repeated. "Never! I've just got some stuff on my mind, that's all. Otherwise I bet I could beat you blindfolded." To make her point, she covered her eyes with her hands and peeked out at him through her fingers.

"It's a bet," Albert said, breaking into a broad grin. Then, with a quick tap, he knocked over his own white king. "Game over," he declared. "Or as they say in chess-speak, I resign. Guess you win after all, Opaline."

The gallant gesture so charmed Opal that for a moment she forgot all about all the horribleness that had happened, all the wrong she had done. Everything seemed new again. Everything seemed possible. She smiled back at Albert and leaned across the chess table. Who knows what she would have done next if she hadn't caught sight of the boys in black suits over Albert's shoulder.

There's Sidney Bristow, she realized, sitting back again as Albert turned to see what had robbed him of her attention. *And there's Jack Baxter.* The short agent squared his shoulders and straightened his dark sunglasses. *But who's the tall, skinny one trailing behind them on the hoverboard?*

xiv*

Who's Your Momma?
{*Which Does Not Translate as "Kiss Me Violet"!}

"DO YOU KNOW THOSE GUYS?" ALBERT BLURTED OUT, the pitch of his voice shooting up an octave.

"Um, no, just from my mom's job," Opal answered, remembering the real reason she was there. *Her old job, that is.* She pushed her hair behind her ears—even though it was already pinned back in barrettes. It was a nervous habit she didn't even know she had.

At least she'd aced the first part of her test: She'd gotten the Black Swans to show up. Bristow and Baxter must have recognized her immediately, but maybe they didn't expect her to have company. They hung back just past the plaza, on the pathway that snaked alongside the river. Big Red propped one foot up on a bench and bent over to tie his sneaker. Little Freckles checked his prominent wristwatch. The skinny kid on the hoverboard skated wide circles around them.

The sight of three boys in somber black suits in the middle of the park in the middle of the day would have been absurd enough, but the sound of a tinkling melody suddenly made it more so.

"The Mister Mushee truck!" Opal recognized the loopy merry-go-round tune. She gave Albert a meaningful look.

Albert stared back at her quizzically.

Opal raised her eyebrows, tilting her head in the direction of the music.

"Oh!" Albert got her gist. "Do you want some soft serve?" he spluttered.

"Chocolate with crunchies," Opal stated, her order at the ready.

"Okay, er, waffle cone?" Albert asked.

"Chocolate-dipped."

"Right . . ." Albert drawled, reluctantly rising from his seat, then standing in place just as conspicuously as the three boys down by the water.

"You're so sweet!" Opal chirped, but she wasn't looking at him. "I'd better go say a quick hi." She got up, too. "Be right back."

Smart as Albert was, he didn't know what he could have said to stop her anyway. He watched her leave, the hem of her mini-dress flouncing above the tops of her knee socks with every step. The ashen clouds from earlier had never delivered on their threat of rain, and he noticed the sky had cleared. Just one oblong puff floated overhead now, a pillow of white against a sheet of blue. Drifting on the wind above the river, it almost appeared to be following Opaline as she walked. Albert bit his lip, frustrated, before starting off in the direction of the ice-cream chimes.

I guess it's not her fault if some other boys—THREE other boys!—just randomly show up at the Gazebra, Albert thought, debating the probability of it. *But Dad says a date is supposed to be with just one person at a time!*

Opal wouldn't let herself look back at Albert. She was on a mission: She had a test to pass and not much time to complete it. It was only when she reached Freckles and Red that, arms folded, she swiftly glanced behind her to make sure her favorite mathlete was far out of earshot.

"Okay, boys," she said in a brusque tone to the Black Swans, "I've only got a minute, so let's cut to the chase."

"Wait," Big Sid demanded, holding up his plump hand like a stop sign. "Where are the pies?"

"There are. No pies." It was Lil' Freckles who said it, though his mouth was set in such a thin grim line that Opal never saw his lips move.

"No pies," she seconded with a shake of her head.

"No way!" Big Red cried out in a combination of anger and woe. "The Smashface post said there'd be pies!"

"The pies. Were just a set-up," Lil' Freckles explained with impatience to his partner. "To get us here. Obviously."

"Not that obviously!" Big Red disputed. He craned his neck, searching one chess table after another with the hungry hope that a pie would magically materialize.

"No pies!" Opal repeated in a terse voice. She could just imagine Scarlet, eavesdropping from the "undisclosed location," laughing her head off at this ridiculousness. "That whole page on Smashface was just a front. I made it up! Who else but a 'First Place Wiener' would friend 'Hot Dog Cobbler'?"

Big Red shrugged. "Lots of people like hot dogs," he grumbled.

"But you didn't realize something was up when yours were the only two requests I accepted?" Opal countered.

"I guess I was too preoccupied by the promise of *Hot Dog Cobbler!*" Big Red barked back, flecks of his spit hitting her forehead.

Opal took a deep breath to keep grounded. She could feel the volts sparking off her shoulders—the breeze from the river bent them sideways. Lil' Freckles' jaw dropped open at the sight, but before he could say a word Opal snapped, "Static electricity!" She sneezed again, then changed the subject. "Who's Slim Shady?"

The boy on the hoverboard was now skating at the water's edge. As Opal got a closer look, she was sure she'd seen him somewhere before.

"New recruit," Big Red huffed at the same time that Lil' Freckles muttered, "Rented suit."

Opal looked from one spy to the other. "Take off those sunglasses," she commanded. And they did.

"Don't worry about the rookie," Freckles said, squinting

in the daylight. "He's just observing in the field. He's not privy. To classified info."

"He's got ties to the supergirl with the purple hair," Big Red piped in. "Could be a valuable source."

That's who he is! Opal realized. She hadn't recognized him at first, camouflaged by his baggy black clothes. But now that the spies mentioned it, Opal remembered the boy rushing to Iris's side after she'd collapsed at her birthday party. "Iris's BF," she said, forgetting for a moment that she was mic'd. "What's his name?"

"Fassbender. Sebastian Fassbender," Agent Baxter replied briskly. "He won't confirm. Or deny. The boyfriend label. But the evidence. Is indisputable."

Just then Sebastian sneezed, causing him to swerve on his board. A less skilled skater would have crashed right into the volunteer in the acid-yellow grass skirt shaking a bucket of grellowy talc into the harbor, but he expertly avoided a collision. Opal shifted her focus from him to the Projekt BeauTekification worker. Although the collar of his tropical shirt was flipped up, it didn't reach high enough to hide

the fishy gills gulping on his neck. Instead of a mustache, rubbery barbels drooped down over his mouth.

The sight of the mutant gave her a chill. It also gave her an opening. She forced herself to smile.

"I didn't realize when you approached me at Synchro de Mayo that you worked for my mother at BeauTek—"

"Technically, we work for Develon Louder." Jack Baxter had put his black sunglasses back on. He slid a stick of gum between his stiff lips. "Your mom was just our handler. *My* mom is our boss."

"Of course." Opal said it as nonchalantly as possible, but her ears were burning. Did Lil' Freckles just say that Develon Louder was his mother? Holy mackerel! *Or holy catfish*, she thought, peering again at the whiskered mutant. She hoped the Ultra Violets' "undisclosed location" was earthquake-proof, because this revelation must have sent out some shockwaves. *And that's got to be a big enough scoop to get me a passing grade!* Opal hoped. The spy boy must have just assumed that her own mother knew this bombshell intel and that she would, too. "She's behind the Beautify Chrysalis Park campaign, right?" Opal asked, to keep the conversation going.

Sidney Bristow snorted but didn't say anything further.

"BeauTekify Chrysalis Park, yes," Jack Baxter bluntly corrected her.

"It doesn't exactly smell pretty!" She tried to make it

sound like a joke, but the strange, sour scent had returned, and it was an effort not to gag.

"You should know," Big Sid said cryptically before scoffing again.

"A temporary environmental side effect. Till midnight Sunday, max." Lil' Jack's comment didn't make things any clearer.

Opal turned her back to the breeze. In the opposite direction, past the chess tables and the Gazebra and out on the street, she could see Albert's sandy-blond head bobbing at the counter of the ice-cream truck. The electricity throbbed in her veins: She was sorely tempted to shoot a horizontal lightning bolt all the way across to him and disintegrate their cones. That would buy her some time. But it didn't seem like the kind of thing an Ultra Violet—an almost Ultra Violet. An Ultra Violet on probation?—would do.

She forged ahead with her questioning.

"So that's why you asked me about mutants at the street fair," she prompted Big Red. "Because you knew they'd be the 'volunteers' behind the project?"

"You're legend among the mutants at BeauTek," he said, for once sounding impressed instead of obnoxious. "The ones who survived the destruction of the Vi-Shush and the ones who got cloned after."

Opal puffed up with pride in spite of herself. Luckily the mic in her barrette couldn't amplify her feelings.

"That's why Sir Louder has us spying on the Ultra Violets," Jack added offhandedly, grinding his gum. "We haven't been able to prove it. Yet. But those girls. Obliterated. Her first generation of mutants. She can't let them derail her new project."

"You call your mother 'sir'?" It was off-topic, but so strange that it caught Opal off-guard. She still couldn't believe that the president of BeauTek was—OMV?—his mom.

"Everyone does," Jack Baxter stated matter-of-factly. "Your mother included."

Should have known that! Opal thought, realizing her gaffe too late. Hoping Jack wouldn't pick up on it, she scrambled to divert his attention. "The Ultra Violets," she said. "That's why I needed to meet with you. So that we combine our efforts. I'm working to infiltrate the group at Chronic Prep, but it won't be easy. Cheri Henderson is a mathematical genius— no doubt she's run every conceivable algorithm to intercept interlopers. It sounds like you might have an in with Iris Tyler, though." She chucked her chin at Sebastian.

"Yeah," Big Red agreed, tugging on the lapels of his black suit jacket. "We'll break him."

"Excellent," Opal commended, drumming the tips of her fingers together in her best imitation of an evildoer. Perhaps too good an imitation. It was as if a taco—a long-ago taco snatched from her lunch tray by a pony-tailed sprite—had snapped in her mind. Because a teensy bit of the bad Opal had returned. Electricity still itched through her system, and a teasing thought tickled her brain. She couldn't resist saying, "Scarlet Jones might be the toughest nut to crack, but . . ."

"But what?" Lil' Freckles tensed, his teeth gripping his gum, as he waited for Opal to explain.

"But I believe she could be compromised," Opal pretended to confide in the salt-and-peppery spy. "The rumor at school is that she's hopelessly in love with . . ."

She paused for effect and looked from side to side as if she were worried someone else might hear.

Jack lowered his sunglasses to stare at her with his navy blue eyes.

"With?" he pressed, his jaw clenched.

"Why, with you, silly," Opal purred. Then she stuck out her hand. "Gentlemen," she ended their meeting, giving each boy a brisk shake before skipping off to catch up with Albert.

No harm was done, really—if anything, a fake relationship between Scarlet and Jack could help the girls counter-spy on the Black Swans. Still, Opal had to smirk. She knew that, wherever the "undisclosed location" was, Scarlet was probably punching holes through its walls right now.

Sometimes, Opal thought naughtily as she accepted her chocolate cone from Albert, *you can have your cake—or ice cream, or hot dog cobbler—and eat it, too.*

15

Not About Boys?

ABOVE THE JOAN RIVER, JUST BEYOND THE GAZEBRA, a sparkling white cloud swung back and forth like a rocking horse in the sky. Scarlet Jones was not literally punching holes through the walls of the Ultra Violets' cloudship. But she was literally bouncing off them.

"'Hopelessly in love'?!" she quoted for at least the third time as she did another frenzied backflip.

Iris and Cheri covered their heads to block against any stray kicks and tried hard not to laugh. Scarlet was so incensed, it just seemed to prove that Opal's prank was on target. Strapped into their seats, the two friends fought to keep down their giggles, tears trickling down their cheeks.

"Scarlet!" Candace called from the cockpit, struggling to maintain cruising altitude while the hyperactive supergirl ricocheted around the aircraft. "Chill. Out!"

In response, Scarlet dropped to the floor and rolled up armadillo-style, burying her head in her knees and then screaming until her throat was raw.

Darth wrapped his tail into a turban around his ears. Scarlet's jeans didn't do much to muffle the noise.

"Scar," Iris said. The sharpness of her scream had stopped Iris from laughing for a second, but as soon as she began talking, she started again. "It's good that—"

"I thought Opal wanted to get back *in* with the Ultra Violets!" Scarlet shouted, cutting Iris off. "This is how she does it? By selling me *out* to Jack Baxter?!"

Iris slapped a hand over her mouth to cover her smile and slowly shook her head. Cheri tried next.

"Scarlet, no, I think what Iris was about to say was that if Lil' Freckles thinks you like him, then we can use that to get closer to him—and to, OMV, his mother!"

"Develon Louder!" Iris exclaimed. "OMV is right."

"But I don't WANT to get closer to him!" Scarlet wailed, pounding her feet on the floor with so much power that now the cloudship bobbed up and down in the sky like a giant's fluffy yo-yo. "Not like that! And definitely not if he is the spawn of Develon!"

"Scarlet, please!" Candace ordered from the pilot's seat, clutching at the gearshift. The swizzle sporks she'd hung from the rearview mirror clinked and clanged.

Iris and Cheri exchanged looks. "Scarlet," Cheri said in the soothing voice she usually used on skittish kittens at the animal shelter where she volunteered. "Are you sure you don't like Jack even a little, alas?"

Scarlet lifted her head from her knees and heaved a

127

deep sigh. Something about her round red face, her long black bangs, and her sprinkling of freckles reminded Iris of a ladybug.

"*Of course* I like him *a little*," she finally admitted through gritted teeth, her eyes clamped shut. "How could I not? He *saved* my *life* at Opal's party! But I can't fake a crush on him to get intel—even if he is Develon's son! That would be . . . wrong!"

Suddenly Scarlet's conundrum didn't seem so funny.

"I could see how that could get complicated," Cheri agreed.

"Yeah," Iris said, then added with bitterness, "though apparently it's not so hard for Sebastian, who 'won't confirm or deny the boyfriend label.'" Jack's blunt words had given her heartburn. She repeated them verbatim. Then started to cry again. Tears of sadness this time.

"Oh, RiRi!" Cheri gushed with sympathy. She threw an arm around Iris's shoulders as Scarlet scooted over on her butt to squeeze her legs. Darth hopped up and burrowed into Iris's lap to provide the group hug with some much needed warm-fuzziness.

After a moment of silence, Cheri breathed, "I'm *sooo* relieved that Philippe the adorbs busboy is not tangled up in this sordid affair!"

"Girls!" Candace commanded, looking through the rearview mirror at the trio. "Get a grip! This is not about boys! It's about Projekt BeauTekification—finding out what it is and putting a stop to it. *Right?*"

"Right," all three girls mumbled, Iris wiping away her tears, Scarlet crawling over to her seat.

"But are Albert and Opal BF and GF now?" Cheri whispered, so that Candace wouldn't hear.

"And on the subject of Opal"—oops, turns out she did hear after all—"what do we think?"

"I think they *are* BF and GF," Cheri announced, now that she didn't have to whisper anymore.

"Not about that!" Candace smacked her forehead, and this time it was her fault that the cloudship glid (*we spell it thusly*) to one side, almost grazing the glowing plasma globe raised high by the Statue of SynchroniCity out in the harbor. "Do we think she proved her loyalty? Did she pass the test?"

"Maybe I'd better not vote," Scarlet muttered as she

buckled her seatbelt. "I don't think I can be very *objective* about it." Although she'd stopped bouncing off the walls, her heart was still beating against her ribs at the thought of ever seeing Agent Jack Baxter again.

"No way," Candace said, slowing down the cloudship until it was idling placidly above the water. She spun around in her pilot's seat to face the Ultra Violets. "This has to be a group decision."

Iris looked out the windshield at the view. The Statue of SynchroniCity gleamed rose gold in the sunlight, her tourmaline eyes glimmering pink and green, her giant orb fizzling with multicolored filaments. Down below, the Joan River flowed. Every now and then Iris caught sight of a fish flashing electric red or blue. More noticeable were the thick patches of phosphorescent sludge coating the surface of the water like lumpy grellowish porridge. And swarming all around Gazebra Plaza were BeauTek volunteers. *Mutants*, Iris thought. *Yuck*. It was difficult to see them clearly from that high above, although their citric grass skirts were hard to miss. If Iris was not mistaken, many of them appeared to be nibbling on ice-cream cones.

"Well," Iris said, turning back to face the other three, "Opal did get the Black Swans to meet with her, like we asked." She began to braid one of her ringlets.

"And she did let us mic the conversation," Candace reminded them.

"The big reveal about, um, Freckles being Develon's son was major?" Cheri delicately suggested as she filed her pinkie finger with a travel-size emery board. Considering Scarlet's freak-out, she was reluctant to bring up the boy's real name again. *Go sit with her,* she encouraged Darth. *You have a very calming influence!*

"It was weird to hear Opal talk about us to the Black Swans," Scarlet said, bending down to pick up Darth, who had just scampered over to her feet. "Even before . . . argh, don't make me go there again." She stroked the skunk's fur, careful not to use too much force, and gently kneaded his little velvet ears.

Iris rushed to fill in the gaps. "Yes, but she didn't tell them anything new. They already knew about"—she swallowed—"me and Sebastian. And Cher came out as a mathematical genius at Synchro de Mayo. I'm more curious about the whole 'midnight Sunday' thing. I wonder what it means . . ."

"That's only a few days from now," Cheri said, "so we'd better find out."

"Is that a *yes* vote, then?" Candace queried. "All in favor of accepting Opal back into the Ultra Violets, raise your hand."

None of the three raised her hand.

"Hmmm." Candace took off her thick black-framed glasses and rubbed the bridge of her nose. "All in favor of *rejecting* Opal, raise your hand."

None of the three raised her hand this time, either.

"When you put it that way, it sounds so mean, Candace," Cheri said.

"I think . . ." Iris was up to her third little braid by now, though each one would start to come undone as soon as she let go of its ends. "I think Opal did what we asked, so we have to let her back in . . . but carefully."

Scarlet and Cheri nodded. It was as close to a unanimous vote as they were going to get.

Candace spun back around in her pilot's seat and shifted the cloudship into FLY gear. "That sounds like a solid plan," she said, steering the aircraft in a wide circle back toward the center of Sync City. "To CVUV?" she asked the girls.

"Actually, Candace," Iris said, "instead of Club Very, do you think you could drop us off by the harbor?"

Stupid Little Sneezes

"AH-AH-AHCHOOOOPSIE!"

It was a dainty sneeze. As dainty as the sneeze she snoze (*that's also how we spell it—okay, maybe just this once*) four years ago in the FLab—the teeny-tiny squeak-sneeze that caused just enough of a change in the air currents to blast a beaker of radioactive goo clear across the room. But that's almost ancient history now, considering this is book three. Today's particular sneeze of Cheri's took place out in the open. Alongside the Joan River.

Greezumtite! Darth thought, his head poking out of Cher's tote bag, his nose twitching.

Candace had piloted the cloudship back over Chrysalis Park, lowering it right above the grassy knoll where the girls so often hung out—most recently for their post–Synchro de Mayo picnic. The teenius figured that a cloud sitting close to a hilltop wouldn't be as suspicious as a cloud dropping all the way down into, for example, a parking lot. With an adios toot of the cloudship's horn, she'd floated off again toward the spires of Sync City while the girls strolled down to the orange-brick promenade, then along the latticework Plexiglas fence, until they reached the cove behind Gazebra Plaza.

"Opal sneezed, too," Iris said, rummaging around in her messenger bag and finding a tissue for her friend. "Did you notice that?" By now, all the little braids she had woven into her hair had unraveled, and the breeze off the river blew a few purple tendrils across her face. She frowned as she gathered up her long locks and looped them into a loose knot. "So did Sebastian," she felt compelled to mention. It was so unfair, she thought, how once you liked somebody, you ended up noticing every little thing about them. Every stupid little thing! Like when they sneezed. They might not even like you anymore, and you didn't *want* to still care about something as trivial as them sneezing. But you still did. So. Unfair!

"I wonder if Opal is off hanging out with Albert," Cheri mused, dabbing her nose. "I wonder where they went after. And what they did!" Her green eyes glittered with the possibilities.

Scarlet didn't say anything. She just tugged on the end of her ponytail and traced her pointed toe across the thin crescent of sand in *ronds de jambe en terre*.

On the touchscreen of her tablet computer, Iris checked the GPS coordinates of a blinking red dot, then bent over the nearest garbage can and reached in. "Here's her mic," she said, Opal's discarded barrette pinched between her thumb and forefinger. She held it up for Cheri and Scarlet to see. "She must have trashed it right after she left the Black Swans." Grimacing, Iris dusted off the hair clip, then dropped it into her messenger bag. After offering a pomegranate lollipop to Cheri and a plum one to Scarlet, she chose blueberry for herself. All three girls unwrapped their candy. Conveniently, they were standing right next to that garbage can—but Iris held on to her small square of waxed paper.

"I guess we couldn't expect Opal to leave the mic on all day," Cheri reasoned, secretly wishing Opal had. That way, Cheri could have eavesdropped on the rest of her date with Albert. After all, she had put *beaucoup* effort into getting those two crazy kids together! Though that's book-one ancient history, too.

"Yeah, who knows what else we might have overheard," Scarlet grumbled. Under cover of her long black bangs, she gave the chess tables darting, birdlike glimpses, but there was no sight of the spy boys, either.

Iris secured her tablet in her bag, then took a few steps closer to the riverbank. "I'm actually glad it's kind of deserted here," she said, crouching down and dipping her fingers into the water. "I wanted to get a close-up look at *this*."

Cheri and Scarlet approached the water's edge, too, Cheri cringing as her platform sandals sunk into the damp sand, Scarlet scattering pebbles and shells with her *jeté* steps. Iris straightened back up and showed the girls her hand. Chalky flecks of yellowy gray fungus stuck to her skin.

"Eww!" Scarlet twisted her features into an ick-face. "What is that, pond scum?"

"I don't know," Iris answered, finding another tissue to wipe off the gunk. "But I noticed it when we were up in the cloudship. There are clumps of this stuff floating on top of the water. It's what the BeauTek volunteer was dumping here."

"And on Synchro de Mayo, too," Cheri said, thinking back to the weird group that she now knew were not tourists at all.

Eeeh-eeeh-eeehsqueech!

"Darth, gesundheit!" Cheri exclaimed as the little skunk shook from the aftershocks of his sneeze. With a clean corner of her tissue, she rubbed his snout. "Let's put on the sweater Iris knit you: I don't want you catching cold out here."

Smelz rotten, he told Cheri as she pulled the purple hoodie over his head.

Again? Cheri asked him. Beside her, Iris took a tentative sniff of the air. Scarlet itched at her nose, then squeezed her nostrils closed with one hand.

"Dud anybuddy else recognize dat scend?" she asked in a dulled, plugged-up voice.

"It's sweeter this time," Cheri said, the realization dawning on her.

"Powderdy." Scarlet nodded, still pinching her nose.

"But with a *soupçon* of brussels sprouts . . ."

"BeauTek is dumping soup in duh ribber?" Scarlet gasped.

Before Cheri could reply that *soupçon* was just a sophisticated way of saying "hint," a raucous splash grabbed their attention. Squinting out toward the Statue of SynchroniCity, the girls spotted three rose-tinted tails slipping below the surface.

"Wud wuz dat?" Scarlet wondered just as three dolphins the color of bubblegum soared up out of the water.

"Pink dolphins?!" Cheri clapped with delight. "Darth, did you see that? Maybe they can hear us!"

While Iris reached for her camera phone and Scarlet watched to see if the three dolphins would leap into the air once more, Cheri sent out her friendliest thoughts. *Hello!* she said. *You look viomazing!*

Thanks! one of the dolphins responded. All three of them popped their heads above the surface of the water and nodded at the girls.

"Id looks like dey're smiling ad us!" Scarlet noticed, smiling back.

Do you know what's up with this stuff in the harbor? Cheri asked. Because who better to ask than the creatures that lived there?

The three dolphins broke into animated chitter-chat.

"What are they saying?" Iris asked as she snapped a few photos.

"They're not sure," Cheri translated, straining to understand. "Something about ants, I think? But that can't be right. Ants don't swim, or do they?"

Before Cheri could ask them any more questions, each of the pink dolphins sprung out of the water and, one after another, flipped a full circle in the air, then dove down again. Waving good-bye with their fins, they swam off.

"Au revoir!" Cheri called after them. "They had to go: They were late for dinner," she explained to Scarlet and Iris. After pondering it for a moment more, she added, "I think I'll call them Sine, Cosine, and Tangent. After the three main functions in trigonometry."

"Catchy," Scarlet snarked as she sprang up in *relevé* to catch a last glimpse.

Cheri waved back until the dolphins were out of sight,

while Scarlet spun nervous pirouettes in place, one hand still clutching her nose. Iris had squatted down at the river's edge again. Floating the wrapper from her blueberry lollipop in the water, she tried to scoop up a thicker sample of the grellowish mold. It was trickier than she would have guessed; each time she got close, the ripples in the water would slosh everything away.

"Umb, Iris?" Scarlet came to a sudden stop in fifth position and tapped Iris on the shoulder with her free hand.

"Give me *one* second," Iris said, the stick of her lollipop gripped between her teeth. "I just want to get a good smear of this sludge . . ."

"Um, Iris?" This time it was Cheri trying to get her attention. Stumbling up to the walkway, she took out her smartphone and quickly keyed in a command to release the wheels of her rollerskates. The sand from the riverbank had coated the soles of her sandals. When the wheels popped out of the platform heels, Cheri hurriedly wiped them in the grass.

"We've got to analyze this stuff," Iris was explaining, all her concentration on the lapping water. "Candace can help us—we can use the equipment at the FLab." Slowly she lifted up the small square of paper, sifting it from side to side like a miner separating grit from gold. "Got it!" she declared, carefully folding up the square and filing it into a pocket of her messenger bag.

"Dat's guud," Scarlet said, now actually grabbing her by the collar and dragging her backward to the walkway, too.

"Hey!" Iris laughed, her legs flailing as she tried to get to her feet. "Take it easy, Tiny Hulk. What's the hurry?"

As she posed the question, she looked up the path and finally saw what the other two Ultra Violets had been staring at.

Racing toward them with the spastic speed of a fish flopping on land, rubbery whiskers slapping like overcooked spaghetti against the shoulders of his hideous Hawaiian shirt, was the gill-necked mutant.

Knots

"SUGARSTICKS!" IRIS SPLUTTERED, THE LOLLIPOP STICK falling from her mouth.

"Time being distance divided by speed"—Cheri swayed back and forth on her skates as she calculated—"I'd estimate that he'll reach us in, oh, twenty seconds."

"We should split up!" Iris had already wrestled her robotic wings out of her bag and was scrambling to shake them open. "He must want the gunk sample. He can't chase all three of us at once, and . . . and fish can't fly. I hope!"

"Fifteen seconds," Cheri counted down.

"I'm not gonna bounce till you're airborne!" Torn between her own fight-or-flight instincts, Scarlet bopped from toe to toe like a boxer.

"No, girls, go!" Iris said, hitching the straps of her wings over her shoulders and fumbling to buckle the harness. "I'm almost ready, I—"

"Ten seconds!" Cheri shouted as Scarlet dropped into a defensive stance and put up her dukes.

"Cover your eyes," Iris commanded, letting go of the loose cords of her harness and raising one hand to the oncoming monster. An ultraviolet aura burst around her as she blasted a blistering lightbeam at the mutant. It hit him square in the shoulder, burning a hole through his hideous floral shirt and deep-frying the ends of two of his damp barbels. With a gurgly groan, the mutant staggered back.

"That's better," Iris muttered, tightening the strap of her harness across her chest, then fidgeting with the click wheel on the control panel.

"Ten seconds again!" Cheri yelped, resuming the countdown. Although his blackened whiskers were affecting his balance, Catfish Face was back on track and lopsidedly barreling toward the girls once more.

Not a second too soon, Iris's wings hummed to life, spreading wide open, the hundreds of vitanium-crystal scales levering horizontal to catch the wind. Haphazardly she shot above the pavement, still struggling to notch the belt at her waist.

"Ultra Violets, seriously, go!" she cried, her hair whipped upright by the vibrating wings. "Recon at CVUV, okay?"

Seeing that Iris was ready for takeoff, the other two girls agreed.

"Fly safe!" Cheri called to her. As Iris zoomed up and off, she spun a half circle on her skates so that she was facing away from the fast-approaching mutant—and Darth's tail was aimed right at him.

"Furi," she instructed her smartphone, "autopilot. Top Speed. Destination: Club Very Ultra Violet." Just as she shoved off, the little skunk let loose a big poot that sharply reeked of tartar sauce.

Catfish Face wheezed and coughed, his gills stung by the acidic spray. He tried to fan the stinky plumes out of his flat fish eyes with his webbed fingers. And as the greasy mayonnaise smoke cleared, he was greeted by the heel of a small black motorcycle bootie.

Doof! Scarlet had jumped three feet off the ground in *sissonne fondu* and then swung her left leg in *grand battement en l'air* to ever so gracefully kickbox the mutant in the mouth. Landing in *grand plié*, agile as a monkey, she rocketed back up and out of the park with a single, spring-loaded leap.

. . .

Not far past the Gazebra's shingled roof, Iris's wings began to falter.

Sugarsticks! she thought again. *Battery's probably low, and I didn't have enough time to solar-power up.* Setting the wings to GLIDE, she shut off the engine completely, steering herself like a kite on the wind currents. As she surveyed the aerial view, she spotted Scarlet by her aubergine ponytail, still airborne herself, bounding over the gates and out of the park. Cheri was ahead of her, almost out of sight, speeding on her roller skates. And the fish-faced mutant was exactly where they'd left him, writhing on the pavement.

And I've still got the sample of gunk in my bag, she thought triumphantly, tilting one wing to maneuver toward the grassy knoll where Candace had dropped them off not that long ago.

It had been, Iris realized, a long day.

And it was about to get a lot longer.

As she started her descent, she noticed that somebody was sitting on the bench. *Our bench*, Iris couldn't help thinking, even though it was a public park and the girls didn't have any official claim to it. Iris didn't want to disturb anyone. But she had to land. It was only as she drifted closer that the figure began to take shape. Slouched in his baggy black suit. Head in his hands. Hoverboard motionless at his feet.

SUGARSTICKS! Iris cried inside. But it was too late. She couldn't change course now. Her feet hit the ground and she stumbled right past Sebastian, her heels plowing skid marks into the grass as she tried to brake to a stop.

At the crest of the hill, Iris came to a standstill. Her heart was pounding so hard she wished that it alone could power her back up and away again. But she knew she had to face Sebastian. It was funny—in a completely unfunny, sort of sickening way: All she had wanted these past few days was to see him, and now that she was about to, it filled her with dread. From the top of her purple head to the tips of her robotic wings. Was he just there by coincidence? Or had he come to the grassy knoll hoping to see her, too?

She paused to dial down the wings, her back to the bench, all the while feeling so strangely that she was both there and not: like she was an actress playing the part of herself. She had no idea how much time was actually passing. Maybe he wouldn't even be there anymore. Maybe he was never there in the first place. Maybe she'd just dreamed this whole scene.

Maybe.

Slowly she turned. Her lowered wings fluttered behind her in the breeze, the vitanium-crystal scales tinkling as if she were wearing a cape threaded with a thousand tiny chimes. Her purple ringlets—terribly tangled again, she was sure, from the flight—rustled above her shoulders. She could feel the radiation rising through her entire body and bet she was blushing valentines. Bands of light from the full color spectrum began to beam from her fingertips. There was no point trying to hide them.

From the bench, where—not a dream—he'd been all along, Sebastian stared up at her with his liquid black eyes. Under the scrutiny of his gaze, Iris knew the periwinkle blue was draining from hers, leaving only the palest violet behind.

"Hi," she barely breathed.

"Hey," he said back.

They stayed like that for what felt like forever, Sebastian seated on the bench, Iris glowing before him.

"I, um," she grappled for what to say next. "I saw you here in the park the other day. I called out your name. I guess you didn't hear me?"

Sebastian narrowed his eyes, observing her with the kind of curiosity he might have had for an exotic animal at the zoo. It was as if he were seeing her for the first time. Taking it all in: the purple hair, the sunrise eyes, the rainbow beams, the violet aura.

The urge to wrap herself up in her crystal wings nearly overwhelmed Iris, but somehow she stood tall.

"You're a superhero," Sebastian said at last, in that same soft voice she had so missed hearing. It wasn't quite an accusation. It wasn't a question, either. But it seemed to demand an answer.

"It . . . it all happened so fast," she stammered. "Well, not really, it actually started four years ago, but then so fast after that." She realized she wasn't making much sense. "I wanted to tell you, but I didn't know yet, I didn't know . . ." She trailed off. There was so much she hadn't known—that she *still* didn't know. How could she ever begin to explain it all to Sebastian?

"The graffiti on the monorail. Painting your name on the dumpster. Your quote-unquote 'performance art' at that girl's party?" His voice broke as he listed the evidence. He tried to laugh it off, but she could hear the anger underneath his words. It stung her like a slap in the face.

"Sebastian, I'm sorry!" Iris said, fighting to keep the quiver out of her own voice. "Please try to understand—I couldn't tell you about my powers! I hardly knew you! And there was so much weirdness going on here in Sync City that I was trying to deal with. But I swear, I never meant to lie to you. I was just trying to protect you from all my crazy while I figured everything out."

"Protect me?" he muttered back, rubbing the palms of his hands up and down on his knees. He attempted to smile, but his lips twisted into something bitter. "I don't need some girl—I don't need anyone—to *protect me.*"

"No, I didn't mean it like that!" Iris took in a quick breath, blinking furiously to keep her tears at bay. Her mind raced to find the right thing to say.

"Through it all," she tried once more, "through all the danger and strangeness here, I was so happy whenever I was with you. When we went on our—" Iris caught herself; she wasn't sure if boys even liked to call them dates. "When we went to the ice-cream café—"

"Yeah, where you fought off a mutant rat!" Sebastian scoffed, remembering it. He shoved the shaggy forelock of black hair out of his eyes, slammed back against the bench, and folded his arms across his chest. "I'm *such* an idiot for not getting it!"

"No! No, you're not!" Iris dared to take one step closer. "No one did!" she said, wringing her hands together so that rainbow beams flickered all over the place. "We kept it a secret. We had to! Even now, even though we've come out in public, I still don't think it's safe, I—" Iris stopped herself again, worried that she'd scare Sebastian away for good if she opened up and told him any more. She felt that same out-of-body sensation as before, of watching herself acting out this drama. A drama desperately in need of a comedic ending.

"You, um, you're hanging with the Black Swans now?" she asked feebly.

"The who?" Sebastian said flatly.

"Oh, that, that's what we call them, of course you wouldn't know that." Iris fluttered her hands as if she could usher away her comment.

"Great. MORE things I don't know," Sebastian replied, raising his eyebrows and flicking his hair back again.

Iris pretended not to notice his sarcasm. "The two boys, uh, Jack and Sid," she explained, using their actual names for once. "You're not friends with Malik and Douglas anymore?" She hoped the fact that she'd remembered his hoverboarding buddies would score her some points.

"No, I am!" Sebastian said defensively, the hair falling forward into his eyes. "Those other two guys, that's—" He paused to inspect his big black suit, as if he'd forgotten what he was wearing. "Never mind, forget it. I guess Sync City is full of supergirls and spies and evil corporations and psycho laboratories, but . . ."

Sebastian stood up. Using way more force than necessary, he stomped the tail end of his hoverboard with one foot to activate it. It buzzed above the grass, waiting for him to hop on.

"Iris, look," he said, although he was looking away, out past the park to the river. "I thought you were cool and everything, but all this, like, Powerpuff, save-the-world stuff . . ." He shrugged, and in that moment Iris could see the sharp edges of his shoulders through the oversized jacket. More than anything, she wanted to lean her head there, against his chest. Maybe listen to his heartbeat. But he wouldn't even face her. "I just, you know, I just want to have fun," he mumbled. "Tag the monorail. Skate."

"You can still do all that!" Iris gave him the warmest smile she could muster. "And we can still hang out! Let's, can we, can we just talk? I'll . . . I'll tell you whatever I can. About this whole Ultra Violet thing."

At last Sebastian looked her in the eyes, searching them for what Iris was sure must have been written in big block letters all over her face. He was close enough now that she could see his long black lashes and a shadow of dark hair across his upper lip.

"You're a superhero," he said again, more tenderly this time. As if that explained everything.

"Yes," Iris said, her throat so tight that it came out as a whisper. "I am. But I'm also just a girl, standing in front of a boy, asking him . . . asking him to . . ." She couldn't finish the sentence. A single tear escaped from her beyond-pale eyes.

"Your hair's all knotty," he murmured, bending his head down to hers and brushing one of her purple ringlets behind her ear. His fingertips lingered on her cheek for a second.

The second passed.

"I gotta bail," he announced abruptly, taking a step back

and turning around. "I don't know, I guess . . . whatever," he tossed over his shoulder. Frozen in place, Iris watched him from behind as he pushed his hair away yet again. But this time he ran the sleeve of his baggy suit jacket across his eyes. "I'll text you, or I'll . . . I'll see you around."

With that—with Iris staring so blindly at the nape of his neck that it must have only been the tears in her eyes that kept her from burning his bare skin—Sebastian stepped onto his hoverboard. And skated away.

Drawing Lines

WHAT HAPPENS AFTER YOUR HEART'S BEEN BRUISED?
When the hurt you'd feared the most has come true? Where
do you go? What do you do?

If you're Iris Grace Tyler, you go back to Club Very UV, just
like you'd promised and just like you'd planned, and you meet
up with your two best friends, and you tell them everything:
everything that you said and everything that he said and
everything you wanted to say but you couldn't and everything
you wanted him to say but he didn't. And you sob so hard,
sometimes into the soft, absorbent fur of a sympathetic
skunk, you sob so much that your chest aches and your breath
comes out in shallow, stabbing gasps. And your friends offer
you gummy bears and chocolate bars but you've lost your
appetite, even for candy. And they tell you how maybe, just
maybe, it's for the best. That okay, he was cute, but maybe,
just maybe, he was also kind of uncool to blow you off not
once but twice, to not be more understanding—maybe? And

they hug you over and over. But eventually they have to go home, so you climb down the spiral stairs alone, back to your room, where you climb into bed even though it's barely even dark out yet, and you bury yourself in your blankets. And then you cry again, even though you didn't think you could cry any more.

And then . . .

The next morning . . .

At the crack of dawn . . .

To the sound of birdsong . . .

You wake up. You open your eyes. And you remember that:

YOU ARE A SUPERHERO.

It's not just some silly label.

It's not an excuse.

It's not a role you play at whim, like childhood dress-up or a costume for Halloween.

No. It's who you are. A superhero. Strong. Fair. Smart. Brave. All the time. Brokenhearted or not. You're a superhero and you've got a city to protect. So you'd better wash your face, even though your eyes are raw red. And you'd better wash your hair; brush out all the knots. And put on your big girl panties.

That's exactly what Iris Grace Tyler did. She did one thing more, too. She wasn't sure why. Cheri was the one who usually wore makeup—just a little, sparkly lip glosses and

154

eco-friendly nail polishes with nonsensical names like Lilac Attack. But the morning after her bad break with Sebastian, Iris was seized by an impulse. And after she'd combed through her signature purple strands until they were smooth and shiny and springing with curls, she picked up a black eye pencil her mom had left behind in the bathroom. And drew a curved line above the lashes of each lid.

Truth be told, what Iris *really* wanted to do with that eye pencil was color in a thick band across her entire face, up to her brows, over the bridge of her nose, back to both temples, so that her bloodshot blue eyes would be set in a ribbon of black. *Just like a heavy metal singer's getup,* she thought. *Or, yeah, a superhero's mask.*

Iris didn't do that. It would have been messy, and it would have messed with the people at school. What was the point of wearing a mask when everyone already knew your secret? So she just drew the two black lines.

And that made her feel a bit better.

After school that Friday afternoon, the four girls walked together from Chronic Prep to the Highly Questionable Tower, aka HQT. Yup, you read right. Four girls. Count 'em! Early that morning, Iris had texted Opaline a cryptic message with a strange request. Then she'd caught up with her at school and, without explaining why, asked her to meet them outside the revolving doors after the last bell. Iris had seemed so matter-of-fact and fierce—even more than she'd been on Monday in the cafeteria—that Opal almost felt like, if she'd said anything but yes, Iris might have snapped and gone supernova on her right there in the hallway. Frankly, it was a bit frightening. Scarlet's raised fist suddenly paled in comparison.

Now, as Opaline Ann Trudeau stood on the threshold of the Fascination Laboratory, aka FLab, she thought back to the last time she was there—four years ago when they'd all been splashed by DNA-altering goo. Maybe she should have been scared by the prospect of returning. Instead she was excited. Nervous, but excited. She'd passed the loyalty test—at least she hoped she had (Iris hadn't said, exactly). She was among the Ultra Violets—even though Scarlet, between pirouettes, had thrown her shade the whole walk over. If Iris hadn't seemed quite so remote, Opal would have reached out and held her hand right then, just like they used to do when they were in kindergarten.

She didn't, though. Because, well, like we said.

"Hi, UVs!" Candace greeted them as they entered the laboratory. "Hi, Opaline!" The erstwhile babysitter welcomed Opal with more warmth than any of the three girls had, even going so far as to imitate Opal's circle-and-two-snaps hand gesture. Opal wanted to die on the spot—how did Candace know about *that*?! And if she knew about that, didn't she also know it was an "old Opal" gesture?

A "bad Opal" gesture, Opal thought. *Although maybe I could rehab it and use it again?*

She smiled back shyly at Candace, hedging on whether she should apologize to her, too. The teenius was sitting on a stool at the stainless steel lab table, wearing a spotless white lab coat and protective plastic goggles over her thick black glasses. Tucked into the goggles' elastic strap was what appeared to be a stainless steel swizzle spork?

"Tell us again why our moms aren't here?" Scarlet demanded, skipping any pleasantries while spinning *chaîné* turns all the way up to the rock-crystal window. Opal wanted to join her there and enjoy the panoramic view of Sync City. But she didn't have to be a scientist to know that Scarlet was keeping her distance—nettled, no doubt, by Opal's lil' fib about her love for Lil' Freckles. So Opal hung back by the lab table instead, her eyes scanning the shelves for all the oddities: test tubes and petri dishes, a squeeze bottle labeled WHOSEEWHATSIT, mason jars with mystery meats afloat in their murky waters. Opal thought she recognized an ear. She shuddered and turned her attention back to the group.

"Your moms," Candace was saying, "are participating in a panel on the global initiative to contain and convert methane gas as a way to combat atmospheric warming."

"Methane gas?" Cheri repeated, fiddling with the dial on a Bunsen burner.

"Cow farts!" Scarlet hollered back from the window, where she was now interpretive dancing. Her modern choreography involved lots of melodramatic tumbles.

"Eww!" Cheri squealed, scrunching her features into an ick-face while Candace cautioned Scarlet to "take it easy up there!"

Scarlet came to a tippy-toed stop. "What?" she said, playing innocent. "That's what methane gas is: cow farts!"

Cheri and Opal looked to Candace for confirmation. Iris, who had half perched on the stool opposite the teenius at the lab table, looked past Scarlet out the rock-crystal window.

"Methane gas does come from decomposing organic matter," Candace admitted with a roll of her eyes. "Such as, yes, bovine flatulence."

"Barf! For serious?" Cheri squealed again while Scarlet

snickered in victory. "Scarlet, how do you even know this stuff?"

Opal guessed it might have something do with Scarlet having three older brothers, but she didn't think it was her place to bring it up.

"Let's get down to business, guys," Iris said, completely nonplussed by the subject of cow farts. She withdrew the folded lollipop wrapper from the pocket of her messenger bag. "Let's analyze this gunk. Opal, did you bring what I asked for?"

All eyes turned to Opaline. After getting Iris's text that morning, it's not that she didn't know this moment must have been coming. But she blushed all the way down to her Peter Pan collar anyway. Reaching into the pocket of her dress, she withdrew what looked like a small glass ball with a squishy pouf on top. Inside, greenish liquid sloshed, black flecks of bracken swirling in the mix.

"Is that—?" Scarlet began, as Cheri backed away.

"Yes, it's L'Eau d'Opes," Iris answered. "It's Opal's mind-control perfume."

"You still have some of that stuff?" Cheri said, dumbstruck—since obviously Opal did. "You kept it, even after everything that happened?"

Opal stared down at her scuffed Mary Janes. "Not to use on anyone," she mumbled. "Just as a kind of, um, memento."

Scarlet glared, her gunmetal eyes shooting back and forth between Opal's hanging head and the bottle of poison perfume in her hands. Cheri made a nervous joke of sorts. "I guess I could understand that," she said. "I guess it's not every day a girl gets a perfume named after her?"

"Hmm, okay." Candace snapped on a fresh pair of latex gloves, strapped on a face mask to cover her mouth, took the sample from Iris, the perfume from Opal, and produced a second spork from the pocket of her lab coat. With precise movements, she used its sharp tines to scrape the pasty grellowish sludge onto a microscope slide. "Don't worry, it's sterilized!" she assured the girls, even though none of them had even thought to ask. Then, on a separate slide, she spritzed a few droplets of the perfume.

The FLab grew quiet, Opal standing self-consciously at the far end of the table, Iris slouched in stony silence, Scarlet aggressively voguing over at the window, and Cheri watching by Candace's side. As the teenius worked, she tried to make more small talk. Her words were slightly muffled by her mask.

"Iris, are you wearing eyeliner?" she asked.

"Yes," Iris replied with just the slightest edge to her voice.

"I think it looks good!" Cheri piped in with a smile: Some of her favorite experiments involved makeup.

"I think it looks good, too," Candace said, focusing as she sandwiched the fungus on the slide by centering a cover slip on top of it. "A bit tough, though?"

"Somebody's gotta be," Iris tossed off.

"Amen to that, sister!" Scarlet shouted, grooving back over to the table in a funky cross-step that involved a shuffle, a dip, and a rotating shoulder shake. It looked really cool. Opal hoped the day would come when Scarlet might show her how to do it.

Lifting the first slide with the tips of her fingers, Candace transferred it to the stage of the microscope. "I saw you talking to Sebastian on the grassy knoll yesterday . . ." she ventured.

"Oh, Candace, seriously?" Iris exclaimed with exasperation. "On the MAUVe cam? It would be nice to have some privacy once in a while!" *Like when a boy is dumping me*, Iris thought. But she didn't say it out loud because she had resolved to be strong. And it's not as if she hadn't already told the whole story, down to the last detail, to Scarlet and Cheri, if not Opaline.

Candace looked up from the microscope at the purple-curled Ultra Violet. Even through her two layers of glasses, Iris could see the compassion in her former babysitter's eyes. She turned away and bit the inside of her cheek to keep from crying again.

"It's not that I mean to spy on you, sweets," Candace said, changing slides. "It's just that I worry about the three of you— the *four* of you," she revised her sentence, "out there, with all that's going on."

Opal appreciated being included in the group. She was just trying to remember what the MAUVe cam was.

"Anyhoo . . ." Candace racked her impressive brain for what to say next. She always found it a tad challenging to be a cheerleader for the girls while still staying "empirically accurate." As an almost-scientist, she considered it an ethical obligation to always be straightforward with them—not to fill their heads with any false hopes or hocus pocus or mushy metaphysical gobbledygook. She'd never forget the time Opal had asked her about the existence of fairy godmothers! Candace didn't believe in fairy tales; she believed in facts and evidence (and also aliens and astrology, because they were equally valid). So she didn't like to say anything she couldn't back up with research. Even though she sensed that was exactly what Iris needed to hear right now.

Candace ran a rubber-gloved hand through her baby bangs and tried again. "Iris, you know better than anyone how things can change," she said. That was certainly true! "And Saturn is at a hard angle to the sun right now, which is causing all kinds of cosmic havoc." That was true, too—astronomical charts could prove it. "So even though it might feel like an end"—this part she was going a bit out on a limb with—"it might really be an . . . *evolution*."

"We don't have to talk about it," Iris said softly, shaking her head.

"Okay." Candace grappled for a more positive way to close the conversation. "But that boy would be crazy to blow you off." Thinking it over, Candace knew this statement was the most empirically accurate of all.

Then she sneezed right into her face mask.

"You too?" Cheri said, passing Candace a tissue from the FLab's sanitized dispenser. "Everyone's been a bit sneezy lately."

"Maybe Snow White cloned her dwarf," Candace deadpanned, giving Opal a wink.

"No, we think it has something to do with this stuff!" Cheri pressed.

Candace propped the protective goggles on top of her head. They left behind a pink outline on her skin, imprinted in half circles under her eyes. "Interesting theory, Cher," she said, tugging down her mask. "I want to run some tests on a smaller sample to analyze its chemical properties—toxicity, flammability, combustion point—"

"You mean to check if it's poisonous, or will catch fire, or explode," Iris said, trying to keep up with Candace's science-speak.

"Exactly." Candace nodded. "But just from observing the slides, I can see the similarities. The spores in the river gunk are, I hypothesize, a condensed version of the same nerve-altering ingredients in the perfume. Airborne, they would definitely be an irritant."

"Spores?" Opal asked, inching a little closer.

"I'd say they're at least partially artificially generated."

Candace leaned back so that Opal could take a peek through the microscope at the squashed mold in extreme close-up. "Though I also detect some organic materials in the composition. A cruciferous vegetable, like broccoli, or cauliflower, or—"

"Or brussels sprouts!" Opal and Scarlet said together. Opal was chagrined, Scarlet angry.

"OMV, Opal, it *is* your perfume again, isn't it?" Cheri cried. "The Projekt BeauTekification mutants are dumping a powdered version in the harbor? But why?" She had left Darth back in Club Very because she thought he might be upset by the presence of Opal. Now she wished he were there. She could have hugged him for comfort.

Opal grimaced. She'd wanted to just walk away from BeauTek, but her bad deeds seemed to be following her. "It's possible that," she said to the four expectant faces looking to her for an explanation, "after the trial batch of perfume was, um, vaporized at my birthday party"—Opal met Iris's pale blue, black-rimmed eyes, but they seemed as faraway as the horizon—"BeauTek could have tweaked the formula."

"Concentrated it into a talc." Candace reached across the lab table to her tablet computer and opened up one of her e-textbooks, though the latex glove was making it hard for her to scroll through the pages on the screen.

"Like baby powder?" Cheri whispered.

"Like crazy powder," Candace said with concern. "Right

now, it seems like it's just a minor irritant. It smells foul, and it makes people sneeze. But"—her rubber-tipped finger paused on a paragraph about time-released toxins—"it may be weakening their immune systems. And if the mind-control chemicals have been condensed in this crazy powder, then BeauTek must have some plan to reactivate them at some point again."

This time Iris did lock onto Opal's stricken look. *"Midnight Sunday, max!"* Both girls quoted back what Agent Jack Baxter had said.

"What, Opal, the entire sixth grade wasn't enough?" Scarlet snapped. "Now BeauTek is trying to poison all of Sync City?"

Good-bye, Gazebra

WHERE IS THE LOVE? CHERI HAD TO ASK HERSELF THAT Saturday afternoon, roller-skating through Chrysalis Park on her way to meet Scarlet.

The luv, the luv . . . Riding shotgun in her shoulder bag, Darth echoed the sentiment, as if they were thinking a duet.

Reminder: Cheri believed in love. She believed that love conquers all. That love is (almost) all you need (nail polish remover being a necessity, too). That love—along with the sun's gravitational pull—makes the world go 'round. If those were clichés, that was just because the power of love had made them universally true. But believe as Cheri did in the L word, Cupid was not exactly cooperating with her designs . . .

Whooz Kewpid? Darth asked, interrupting her thoughts.

A flying baby who shoots an arrow through your heart to make you crush on someone, Cheri explained as she skated.

Darth squeaked with alarm. *Iz another mutant?!* He

wondered what stink he should use against a winged baby packing a crossbow.

Cheri didn't respond. She was too wrapped up in her analysis, mentally reviewing the status of all the boy-girl combos she could think of. Kind of like a reality TV results show in her brain. *First, I tried to set up Albert with Opal*, she mused. *And he fell for me instead—major fail, alas. Though those two finally seem to be friendly?* She smiled, but her satisfaction only lasted a second. *Now, because Iris is all bummed out over one borderline Black Swan, I'm sneaking around to help Scarlet, who is smitten with another: a spy who wants to bring down the Ultra Violets!*

The romantic intrigue was so complicated she needed a color-coded flow chart to keep track of it all. Her hair took on a magenta tint as she set one up in her mind. She filed it away when she spotted Scarlet up ahead.

Cheri slid to a halt on her platform skates as she reached her.

"Read the invite again?" It was the first thing Scarlet said. Brimming with energy, she triple-backflipped right there on the grass.

"Hello to you, too," Cheri quipped as Scarlet landed upright beside her.

The petite-est Ultra Violet raised her eyebrows beneath her long bangs and gave her friend an imploring look.

"By now I can recite it by heart." Cheri clutched her hands

to her chest and stared up at the sky as she said, *"Dearest Scarlet, it has recently been brought to my attention that you are 'hopelessly in love' with me."*

"Shut. Up!" Scarlet bounced three feet off the ground, and Cheri had to swerve in a speedy half circle to avoid a superpowered shove that would have sent her *bang, zoom!* all the way to the river. "It does *not* say that!" Scarlet huffed, planting her feet back on the sidewalk in a defiant second-position stance.

"Temper, temper, Scar!" Cheri chided, pulling out her smartphone by the fuzzy green rabbit ears of its knitted case. She opened up the controversial text message with the tap of one lilac-lacquered fingernail. "Furi," she directed, "read invite."

For fun, just before the digital assistant could begin, Cheri activated another app.

"R-r-reading," Furi reported back, her robotic voice filtered through autotune so that she sounded like an overproduced pop singer:

no more *b-b-black*-and-white *rrrred*.
gazebra @ 4:00 p.m. *sa-sa-saturday.*

"Oh, you're *ha-ha*-hilarious today!" To Cheri's giggles, Scarlet imitated the autotune, even though the techno message had made her sway in place. *"No more black-and-*

white," she repeated for the umpteenth time. "Do you think he was talking about his hair? You know, the way it's salt-and-peppery?" Scarlet tugged on the end of her dark, shiny ponytail. It once would have been unthinkable for her to voice such a boy-centric question. Even now it made her cheeks hot. But she felt like she could risk being embarrassed in front of Cheri. Scarlet knew the girl pretty much lived for this kind of gooey stuff.

"Mmmaybe," Cheri said, her waves glowing magenta again as she gave it her full consideration. "Though, in general, I'm not sure that boys text about their hair very much. Do your brothers?" Cheri just had a baby sister, which wasn't much help in the sibling department.

"Based on how much they hog the bathroom in the mornings, probably!" Scarlet scoffed, posing one foot and then the other in *cou-de-pied.*

"Still, it seems très random that Jack would suddenly send you a message about his hair. An anonymous message!" Cheri remembered. "All kidding aside, we don't actually *know* it's from him, Scar. And we don't know it's to you, either. We both got the text. Maybe 'red' means me, because of *my* hair? Or that it's from his partner, 'Big Red' Sidney Bristow?"

"But 'red' could also mean Scarlet, right?" Scarlet said hopefully, dropping her hands down from second position and jumping up in *relevé*.

"*C'est possible.*" Cheri skated a full circle around Scarlet as she balanced. "Oh, why must boys be so oblique!" she bemoaned, borrowing a term from geometry. "Why won't they just come out and say what they mean!" She thought back to Iris's retelling of her painful conversation with Sebastian, all his false starts and sentence fragments, all so open to interpretation. "Maybe the text message isn't even *from* a boy!"

She and Scarlet both flopped down on the nearest bench, dejected by that option.

"No, it has to be," Scarlet argued, finding a piece of cinnamon gum in the pocket of her jeans and folding it in half. "Can't we trace it later, back in Club Very?"

"We can try," Cheri said, tearing off her share of the gum stick. "It's probably protected by some sort of spyware, but maybe we can hack it." Suddenly she grinned, and her green eyes lit up. "It is all kinds of delicious, isn't it? The mystery of the secret text message? It's irresistible!"

Scarlet exhaled an exaggerated breath, puffing up her cheeks like a freckle-faced chipmunk. "It's stressing me out," she said. "I am *not* going to lie to Jack!" She gave her shoulder a stern thump, as if she was fighting with herself. "And I am *not* 'hopelessly in love' with him, either! Ugh, even if I forgive

Opal for everything else, how can I ever forget she said *that*? But I'm not going to let Jack roll out Projekt BeauTekification, no matter what." She paused to stretch the thin membrane of gum with the tip of her tongue till she poked a hole through it. "I only wish Iris were with us," she said. "But if Sebastian—"

"We don't know one hundred percent for sure that he's with the Swans," Cheri rushed to say before Scarlet could finish the thought. As a believer in love, she wasn't giving up on Iris's Graffiti Boy just yet.

"Cher, he was wearing the black suit . . ." Scarlet reminded her. Scarlet wanted to believe in love, too—just as much as Cheri. But growing up with those three older brothers had given her a more realistic, sometimes more skeptical, opinion of the opposite sex.

"Anyway, you're right, it's just as well Iris isn't here—just in case Sebastian is," Cheri admitted. "So she's off developing gunk antidotes with Candace. And we're . . . doing recon!"

"Recon, exactly," Scarlet readily agreed. "Observing the enemy. Totally legit." Borrowing a brush from Cheri's bag, she fixed her bangs. "How do I look?" she asked, *jeté*ing up from the bench.

"Viomazing," Cheri said, clicking a quick picture on her smartphone. "All that's missing is . . ."

"Let me guess." Scarlet passed the brush back to Darth, who nudged up a berry-colored tube with his snout. "Lip gloss." She screwed the cap off, swabbed some of the rosy-red cream on her pinkie finger, then swiped it across her mouth.

Cheri tapped her phone again and held it above her head.

"Vio-may-ay-ay-zing!" Furi sang out in robotic autotune.

Scarlet adjusted the neckline of her loose top, but it just slipped off one shoulder again as she set off down the pathway in *pas de basque*. "C'mon!" she called back to Cheri. "It's almost four o'clock!"

They knew they were close to the harbor when all three of them—Darth included—sneezed.

"Gesund . . ." Scarlet started to say, but her glossified mouth dropped open as they rounded the bend toward Gazebra Plaza. At the far end of the lawn, fresh as a newly dug grave, was a construction site. Mud-splattered backhoes tore their steel teeth through the pavement. Dusty dump trucks carted off chunks of dug-up cement. Bulldozers with caterpillar wheels pushed back mounds of dirt. And between all the vehicles bustled a crew of Projekt BeauTekification volunteers, their hardhats the same nauseating yellow as their ridiculous grass skirts. They were carrying shovels, or jackhammers, or ice-cream cones. Parked in its usual spot, the Mister Mushee truck was doing a brisk business, its jingle tinkling through the air in weirdly cheerful contrast to all the demolition noise.

Off to one side, stacked in a pile, were a bunch of black-and-white planks. Nails jutted out of them at awkward angles; Scarlet and Cheri could see the splintered wood beneath chips in the paint. Its supporting posts ripped out like rotten teeth, all that remained of the Gazebra was the shingled black-and-white roof. It sat atop the flattened platform of the stage, a collapsed soufflé.

"No more black-and-white!" Cheri gasped. "It was the Gazebra! BeauTek destroyed the Gazebra!"

"But . . ." Scarlet spluttered, "now where will I debut my new dance routine? And where will we light the holiday tree in winter? Or have Synchro de Mayo *next* year?"

Scarlet's nervousness at possibly seeing Jack had been brusquely bumped to the back of the line of her emotions.

Anger had muscled its way to the front. She was a heartbeat from bursting ahead and beating up the first suspect to cross her path, be it Sebastian, Big Sidney, or Lil' Freckles himself. But before she could bolt, Cher caught her by the collar and yanked her back.

"Hold up, Captain Impulsive!" she hissed, skating in reverse, dragging the feisty Ultra Violet behind the trunk of a fluffula tree. Scarlet squirmed under Cheri's grip. Cher could feel her nails breaking from the strain. With Scarlet's superstrength, there was no way Cheri could contain her. Her only hope was to use math. "Take a deep breath and count to ten! It's too late to stop them now, and we're outnumbered. Let's stick to the plan. Do some spying of our own."

Rather than count, Scarlet gave herself ten quick slaps on the arm. Then, just once, she stomped her foot on the grass. The tremors that resulted reached all the way over to the stack of striped planks, shaking a few off the top. "All right!" she agreed reluctantly. "But let me go!"

"Pinkie-swear you won't run out there and *grand battement* someone!" Cheri demanded. The fabric of Scarlet's sweatshirt had almost slipped from her grasp.

"I promise!" Scarlet swore. To prove it, she held up a pinkie finger. "Ka-pow," she grumbled. "Or not."

Cheri touched her pinkie to Scarlet's, and ultraviolet sparks burst from their fingertips. "Blammo," Cheri murmured

174

back. "Or not." Then she let Scarlet go—or maybe she just lost hold of her shirt. As Cheri hid behind the tree trunk, Scarlet squirreled up it and into the branches for a better view.

Darth scampered out of Cheri's tote bag to follow her.

From above or below, though, girls and skunk saw the same thing. Supervising the crew were two high-heeled women in hardhats. One was skeletally slender: Her wasp-waisted suit appeared impervious to all the dust swirling around her, and her six-inch stilettos somehow didn't sink in the dirt.

"Develon Louder," Scarlet whispered down.

The other woman had a squatter, broader build. Her face was flushed pink from exertion. Strands of root-beer-brown hair stuck to her sweaty forehead. Clumps of mud caked up over her shoes like crusted anklets.

"And Mayor Blumesberry," Cheri whispered up. "Scar!" she quietly called. "Check out who's behind the wheel of the steamroller."

Scarlet peered through the frilly red leaves of the fluffula tree, focusing in on the driver. Protected by the vehicle's cab, he hadn't bothered with a hardhat. Scarlet would know that frizzled orange flattop anywhere.

"Big Red Bristow," she spat, right as he flattened a bike rack.

Darth let out a squeak and pawed at Scarlet's elbow. When she looked at the little skunk beside her on the branch, he pointed his tail.

"Cher!" Scarlet *psssted*. "Sebastian, nine o'clock!"

As smart as Cheri was at math, it took her a moment to remember where the nine was on the dial—since most watches were digital now. But as she glanced over to the left, she spotted him. Shoulders hunched, he was hiding behind a grove of trees, too, surfing in and out of them on his hoverboard. He wasn't wearing a hardhat. Or, to Cheri's relief, a black suit.

"WTV!" Scarlet blurted out, grabbing Cher's attention. If there hadn't been such a ruckus coming from the construction site, she was sure someone would have heard.

"What?" she called up to Scarlet just as she realized Darth was racing back down the trunk. He made a nosedive into his bag. "What is it?"

Then Cheri's eyes fell upon what Scarlet must have seen. Standing beside Develon Louder—his mother—was Agent Jack Baxter. His black suit, just like hers, seemed defiantly spotless despite all the construction dust. Protective goggles covered his eyes, protective orange earmuffs covered his ears, and a bright yellow hardhat covered his hair—which, Cheri imagined, was just as salt-and-peppery as ever.

But that wasn't what had caused Scarlet to cry out.

No, what was most disturbing about this freakish family portrait was that Jack, in his sleek black suit and shiny safety gear, was gripping a slim black canister, his thumb poised above a round red button at its top.

"Is that—?" Cheri stammered.

"A detonator," Scarlet grimly confirmed.

Cheri stuck her fingers in her ears. Scarlet held her breath. Darth—even though he was already in the bag—shielded his eyes with his tail. As the two girls watched from their hiding spot, Jack looked up at his mother. Through the clear plastic panel of her megabucks handbag, she looked down at her son. Silver chignon bobbing like a bell, she gave a single, decisive nod.

Jack nodded back. Pressed the button in the palm of his hand. And the roof of the Gazebra blew to smithereens with a muffled *boom*.

Cheri still had her ears plugged, and the explosion drowned out Scarlet's words. But Scarlet didn't care. She said them anyway.

"That is *it*, Jack Baxter!" she vowed, shaking her small fist at the Black Swan through the fluffy red foliage of the tree. "I'm now hopelessly at WAR with you!"

The Morning After
{*Two Kisses?!}

IT WAS RIDICULOUSLY EARLY FOR A SUNDAY MORNING.

But when you're a superhero . . .

And when an evil cosmeceutical corporation is in cahoots with the kooky mayor, seemingly scheming to somehow enslave the city's entire population by glutting the river with time-sensitive, mind-controlling talcum powder . . .

And when your love/hate crush is making cherished, black-and-white-striped pieces of public property go boom, well . . .

Sometimes you have to get up early. Even on a Sunday. Even when you didn't sleep a wink the night before.

Scarlet was the first to arrive at Club Very Ultra Violet. She'd had a restless night for sure, cancan-kicking off her sheets as she dreamt terrible dreams of Agent Jack Baxter in a garish yellow hardhat, his eyes hidden by his black sunglasses, slimy catfish whiskers hanging down around his mouth, same as on that mutant's. Except Jack's were black-and-white, like his hair. And like the Gazebra he'd blasted to smithereens. As he tilted his face closer to hers, the moist barbels coiled and twitched, reaching out like tiny tentacles to suck the freckles off her cheeks.

She woke up screaming.

The brother in the bedroom to the right pounded on the wall and shouted for her to shut up. The brother in the bedroom to the left knocked three times and asked if she was okay. The brother across the hall didn't say anything. He still had his TV on. Scarlet could hear its low rumble of dialogue and then, clearer, the commercials for laundry detergent and aeroscooter insurance when the volume automatically bumped up.

"Sorry!" she softly called, hoping her parents had slept through her cries and wouldn't come to check on her.

In the dark, she gathered up her blankets from the floor and tried to straighten out her bed. But as soon as she fell back into another fitful sleep, she kicked off the sheets all over again. At the first sign of dawn, when slivers of white-gray light outlined the blinds covering her bedroom windows, she gave up and got up and quietly got dressed.

Dew beaded the grass in her backyard. As Scarlet adjusted her robo-hummingbird wings for takeoff, the wind from the vibrating vitanium scales blew the verdant blades by her feet flat against the ground.

Sneezing just once during her ascent, she reached an altitude above the immediate airstream of the powdery pathogens. With the sun's orange promise on the horizon but the inky blue vestige of the previous night still high in the sky, the view was breathtaking, and the cool air revived her, at least a bit. Since it was still so early, she flew a meandering loop-de-loop around the city, circling the carved crystal FLaboratory atop the Highly Questionable Tower; gliding over the oddly egg-shaped, eerily empty, green-glassed Chronic Prep building; and then soaring past Chrysalis Park, with its riverside promenade, square of chess tables, and freshly excavated construction pit formerly known as Gazebra Plaza (!).

The image of Jack pressing the button and the pavilion going kablooey flashed through her mind, and she shuddered in midair.

Even that early in the morning, the Mister Mushee truck was singing its spooky tune. It echoed throughout the empty park. Even that early, the place was swarming with BeauTek's weird, twig-thin workers in their hideous luau uniforms. So many workers, Scarlet began to wonder if they were multiplying right on the spot. She had no idea where they were all coming from, or what, exactly, they were. With worry, she observed the harbor just beyond. By now a thick scum of congealed crazy powder swirled on the surface, plump with all the water molecules it must have absorbed. From Scarlet's aerial vantage point, the sludge appeared to be seething, little grellowy bubbles boiling up and bursting like a simmering poison soup.

Oh, that can't be good, Scarlet thought, cutting short her joy-fly. *Not good at all!*

She darted up and away from the disturbing scene with such haste that she bumped right into the Statue of SynchroniCity's giant plasma orb. Luckily she didn't shatter it. But it did light up with a frenzy of crackling currents, purple, red, and blue, from the stimulus of her crash. "Sorry, Lady!" she said aloud to the giant sculpture's placidly smiling face.

After that near miss, she made a beeline for the violet beacon that blinked on the rooftop of Iris's sleek apartment building—and Club Very Ultra Violet.

She let herself in, tiptoeing down the spiral iron staircase and barely rustling the beaded curtain into the room. From his potpourri pillow, Darth lifted one eyelid, then greeted her with a lazy wave of his tail before settling back to sleep. In the silence, Scarlet tried to still her mind by repeating a basic ballet barre routine at the clubhouse's massive flower window.

But even this reminds me of Jack, she couldn't help thinking. Because that window was where he'd first spied on her.

"You couldn't sleep, either?" Cheri whispered when, fifteen minutes later, she, too, pussyfooted down the spiral staircase and into the clubhouse. She hung up her hummingbird wings next to Scarlet's, then tiptoed over to give Darth a good-morning kiss on his soft, sleepy, purple-striped head.

"Nightmares," Scarlet stated simply.

"Me too." Cher draped herself across the marshmallow sofa with a sigh. "I dreamed of Mayor Blumesberry's big 3-D head looming over Sync City like a parade float on the loose."

"Yikes," was all Scarlet said. She didn't feel like going into details about her bad dreams, so she switched to small talk instead. "I'm trying to dance quietly so that I don't wake up Iris downstairs."

When Cheri didn't respond, Scarlet looked over from the sunny window to see that she had dozed off on the couch. Darth pitter-pattered over from his pillow, hopped up, and snuggled into her side.

A dull *thud* above caught Scarlet's attention. At the sound of steps on the roof, her supersenses started tingling in spite of how tired she was. Fists raised, she *chassézed* toward the stairwell just as Iris slipped through the strands of beads. She was wearing the black eyeliner again. Her purple ringlets were once more in knots. She carried a flimsy bakery box, balancing a cardboard tray that held four large paper cups on top. Scarlet could see the steam escaping through the slots in their lids.

"Hey, girl, don't *battement* me!" Iris said with a half smile, surprised to find Scarlet already in CVUV. And Cheri, too. "I got your text, but I didn't think you'd be here so early. I haven't really been sleeping well—"

"Me neither," said Scarlet, taking the tray from Iris and placing it on the black marble table.

"So I figured I'd fly down to Tom's Diner," Iris explained as she hung up her wings beside Cheri's, "and pick us up some lattes."

"Coffee?" Scarlet lifted the cup labeled with an *S* and took a tentative sip. "Ooh, strong!" she said, making a mild ick-face. "And a bit bitter." She took another sip, this time pausing to savor the milky brew. "But good!" She grinned. "I can taste the cinnamon. And the caramel sauce."

"A butterbeer latte. The sassy waitress thought you'd like it." Iris half smiled again. "She says hi, btw. Mine's got vanilla-lavender essence. Cheri's is peppermint . . ."

"And?" Scarlet eyed the fourth cup.

"Opal's is a mocha," Iris said. Just then her smartphone buzzed. "That's probably her now." She glanced at the screen. "Uh-huh, in the lobby. I'll go get her."

The stimulating scents of the coffees roused Cheri again. She joined Scarlet at the table, rubbing the sleep from her eyes. "Yummy," she said, breathing in the peppermint. "What's in the box?"

"What else?" Iris tossed over her shoulder as she started down the stairs. "Pie. Apple crumble. Perfect for breakfast."

"Speaking of which," Cheri called after her, "by any chance did you see that cutie pie busboy Philippe at the diner? He makes *me* crumble!"

The very first thing Opaline noticed when she entered Club Very Ultra Violet for the very first time was her black pearl collar on Skeletony, the old FLab skeleton Scarlet had salvaged from BeauTek's Vi-Shush laboratory back when Opal was leading the mutant troop. Cheri had won the collar in a poker game in the boys' room at Chronic Prep back when she was plotting to zombotomize their entire class with BeauTek's toxic perfume. The same perfume that, in powder form, was now festering in the river.

Opal sighed inside. *The past*, she thought, *is never dead. It's not even past.*

Then she drank a deep, slow sip of her mocha latte.

"This place is *viomazing*, guys," she said. The word felt clumsy on her tongue—like it belonged to a foreign language she wasn't sure how to speak. But she tried it out anyway. Sensing the eyes of the other three Ultra Violets (and one very wary skunk) on her, she made a quick tour of the clubhouse, taking in the squishy silver beanbag, the white marshmallow sofa, the pink shag rug, and the fabulous flower-shaped window. She stopped to linger on the three sets of robotic hummingbird wings, hanging side by side just like their coats in the kindergarten closet years ago. The wings were so beautiful—and so powerful, each pair made from hundreds of shimmering, indestructible scales. The way the iridescent colors were arranged, they almost looked dip-dyed: starting off pale at the shoulder blades and then deepening at the tips. Even if she hadn't already seen the girls wearing them when they'd flown in to come out at Synchro de Mayo, it would be easy to guess which pair belonged to which Ultra Violet.

The burgundy-gray combo is so Scarlet. Opal swallowed another sip of her latte. *The shades of pink are perfect for Cheri. And the electric blue–royal purple fits Iris to a T.*

Opal wanted to reach out and brush her fingertips across the wings, hear the tinkling sound they made when all the tiny discs touched. But the other girls were watching, and they would think that was weird. She resisted the urge and turned around to face them instead.

"Okay," she said, walking back toward the table, "let's get down to business." For emphasis, she snapped her fingers twice. She didn't sweep her hand in the full letter *O*—that would have been overkill. But she did snap *slightly* up high, and *slightly* down low. She was hoping to get some of her swagger, some of her mojo, back. By the shocked expressions on the other girls' faces, though, she could tell she'd made a, er, fo pas.

"Too soon?" she asked meekly.

"Too soon!" the three Ultra Violets chorused back.

Hours later, the coffee cups were long empty and the apple pie long gone. Scattered across the table were smartphones and notebooks. The screen of one laptop was filled with complicated chemical equations. The screen of another featured the latest news about movie stars and boy bands— during their serious strategy session, they took the occasional well-deserved celebrity-gossip break. And on the screen of a third laptop, Darth kept pressing PLAY on a GoobToob channel and snickering to himself.

"What's so funny?" Cheri asked, chucking him under the chin and making him chortle more.

Grumpy Skunk gif, he chittered back, pawing at the PLAY button again.

Sitting sideways in the fuzzy orange egg chair, Iris studied the blueprints on the screen of her iCanvas. "Opal, these are incredible," she said. "I can't believe we got them."

„⊥oⱹϱllʎi„ Scarlet said, upside down in a handstand on the pink shag rug. Although she still had plenty of reservations about Opal joining the Ultra Violets, she had to give the girl mad props for the major intel she'd just provided on BeauTek's plans for Gazebra Plaza. "It's just like when they downloaded the data maps to the Death Star from R2D2 in *Star Wars!*" Scarlet knew that was kind of a throwback reference, but sooner or later *everybody* sees the original *Star Wars*. Thanks to her brothers, Scarlet had seen it about ten times.

On the outside, Opal kept up a cool façade. Inside, she beamed at the praise. "I remembered BeauTek had plans for the river," she said, tracing a finger along the white veins in the black marble tabletop. "My mom and I talked about them the night after my birthday party . . ."

At the mention of the calamitous party, all four girls shifted uncomfortably. Iris kept her eyes on her tablet; Opal twisted her hands up inside her sleeves; and Scarlet decided it would be a good time to drop down and practice her Pilates plank pose. Cheri, filing her already short nails, tried to move the conversation along.

"It's awesome that you could access BeauTek's systems

externally, Opal," she said, her green eyes still streaming with computer codes. "It made hacking into those confidential files a breeze!"

"You'd think they'd have deleted my mother's account by now," Opal mumbled, even though, again, the pie was long gone. "But apparently not."

"In a big company like BeauTek, corporate security must be a constant source of vulnerability, alas," Cheri commented. She didn't see Scarlet's quizzical expression because Scarlet still had her head down in plank pose. And Cheri had her own head down, anyway, concentrating on painting her nails with a fresh coat of her favorite sparkly nail polish.

"Anything else you can remember, Opal?" Iris asked, scrolling through screens on her tablet. "Anything that might be useful?"

Clouds passed over Opal's brown eyes as she thought back. "This might not mean much . . ." She hesitated.

"You never know," Iris encouraged her. "What is it?"

"My mother did say"—Opal braced herself for Scarlet's reaction—"that she thought one of the two spy boys was a double agent."

"Ha!" Scarlet scoffed, beginning a vigorous set of push-ups. "I doubt it, seeing as we just witnessed them blow up the Gazebra!"

"I still can't believe they tore down the Gazebra," Iris said, shaking her tangled tresses. "Or, I mean, I can *now*. Now that

I've seen these blueprints and we know BeauTek is planning to put this . . . this colossal contraption in its place!"

"Though we still don't know who tipped us off about it," Cheri added, using her ongoing manicure as an excuse not to make eye contact with Iris. "It could have been Sebastian who sent that text message," she dared to say.

Iris was silent.

"He wasn't wearing the black suit yesterday?" Cheri attempted again.

Still Iris wouldn't touch the subject of her conflicted Graffiti Boy. With her rhinestone stylus, she tapped the screen of her tablet, then swung her legs around and stood up. "Okay, I've just sent you all individual instructions based on what we discussed."

"Got it," Opal and Cheri said together as both of their phones swooshed with the sound of an incoming message.

"And you copied in Candace on the plan, right?" Scarlet asked, completing her one hundredth push-up.

"Totes." Iris nodded. "She texted back that she's out now, um, having a ball?" she joked.

"Out *cracking* a ball," said Cheri, "pinkies crossed."

"I nearly cracked it this morning," Scarlet recalled. "Purely by accident."

Iris glanced through the massive flower window to the twilight skies beyond. "But Candace will be here with the cloudship tonight."

"Projekt BeauTekification," Scarlet declared, springing to her feet, "prepare for your wreckification."

"Prepare," Iris said, nearly smiling for real this time as Cheri held up her bottle of nail polish and rattled it like a maraca, "for the Lilac Attack."

Pluck, Oooh!

"JUST A PINCH, THAT'S ALL YOU'LL FEEL, I PROMISE.
Just a bit of plasma, that's all I'll take. And it's to save the population from mind control, so it's for a *really* good cause! Okay, Lady SynchroniCity? We cool?"

Candace had piloted the cloudship straight up to the face of the statue in the harbor. Lady SynchroniCity's watermelon tourmaline eyes—clear carnation pink at the center, deep forest green around the rims, and a full four feet in diameter—gazed back benignly through the windshield at the teenius. Being (nearly) a scientist, Candace felt a tad silly talking to a statue. But only a tad. She knew that, lovely as Lady SynchroniCity was, she was still an inanimate object, molded from molten rose gold, with no more power to reply than the stainless steel swizzle sporks Candace collected as odd talismans. Yet Lady SynchroniCity was not some commonplace kitchen utensil! She was a monument. She symbolized so much—about strength and creativity and . . .

"And the fundamental connectivity of all things: That's synchronicity!" Candace proclaimed, reminding herself of the founding principles of the city that she and the Ultra Violets were scrambling to save. Considering how important those principles were, Candace believed it was only right that she explain to the guardian statue just what she was about to do.

"So, um, namaste." Candace brought her palms together and bowed to the statue's hypnotic eyes. "Coddington out." (She wasn't sure how else to wrap up the one-way conversation.)

Candace shifted the cloudship into reverse, slowly backing away from the sculpture's face. She stalled briefly to survey the scene. *Lady SynchroniCity will have a perfect view of the action later tonight*, she thought. Candace could see the curdled clumps of poison powder undulating on the surface of the water as it lapped against the riverbank. A few Projekt BeauTekification workers, in their heinous yellow hardhats and goofy hula skirts, were still scattering the stuff. Past the cove, Chrysalis Park was almost empty. Due to the recent sneeze epidemic, more and more people were staying home, afraid of catching "the flu" that suddenly seemed to be infecting the entire city. *If only they knew that a foul powder is what's really causing their achoos.* Candace changed gears again. *And that by Monday they'll all have lost their minds to it—unless we catalyze the stuff in time.*

Had anyone been watching that particular cloud in the Sunday evening sky, they might have done a double take when, like an aerial elevator, it shot upward in a strict vertical line. Candace reached the statue's raised orb in a matter of seconds. Now she idled the cloudship alongside it, the aircraft's vapors veiling the light the same way fog can obscure the moon. The orb's constantly flickering colors still glowed purple, red, and blue through the brume. They lit up the inside of the cloudship, too. If Candace hadn't had such a crucial mission to complete, she would have taken a moment to groove there in her own private dance club.

Actually, she did. Groove, that is. Get down with her bad self. Just for a minute! It helped to get the nervous energy out of her system before she hunkered down to the painstakingly precise gig at hand.

Candace cracked her knuckles. Buckled herself back into the pilot's seat. And adjusted the microscopic lens she'd built into her glasses. "Let's do this."

With the press of a button on the dashboard, the curved windshield pane of the cockpit slid up, leaving nothing but air between Candace and the Statue of SynchroniCity's pulsating plasmatic orb. Flicking a few more switches, she redirected the pipes of the exhaust system so that the mist the aircraft was constantly recycling didn't waft into the cabin.

"Next"—Candace positioned her fingertips on the rubbery-smooth surface of a small trackball protruding like a pimple from the console—"comes the tricky part."

As she began to maneuver the ball, a thin, multi-jointed extension with a thicker, multi-tooled attachment on its end unfolded from the blunt nose of the cloudship. It stretched out until, ever so slightly, it made contact with the orb's crystal surface. That faint touch alone sent the plasma filaments into a frenzy, twitching with such spasticity that Candace shielded her eyes while her glasses automatically darkened.

Plasma orb blinking like a billboard before her, Candace tapped an application on her tablet, and the multi-tooled end of the robotic arm opened up like a lotus blossom, revealing a different implement on each metal petal. There was the screwdriver, the skeleton key, the earring-hole-puncher, the cheese knife. Candace guided the trackball again, rotating the attachment until the petal containing the laser-sharp tines of a spork was in the center position. "And drill . . ." she murmured, activating that icon on the app. The spork began to spin, carving a clean-edged disc no bigger than a pencil's eraser out of the crystal.

"I've cracked the orb." Thumbing back the trackball, Candace retracted the spork. The tiny plug of cut crystal clung magnetically to its tines. "Now to pluck the plasma."

Despite the cool air passing through the open

window, sweat began to bead across Candace's forehead. Cautiously maneuvering the trackball, splitting her glimpses between the actual orb and the live video of it on her tablet screen, she rotated the multi-tooled attachment another few notches. "It's just like playing *Operation*," she observed aloud, making sure her next implement—a slim pair of tweezers—was expertly aligned before she inched it through the newly made hole. "Or that carnival game when you try to pick up a stuffed animal prize with a crane. Now come to mama . . ."

But the plasma filaments protested the intrusion of the tweezers even more than they had the drilling of the spork. They crackled like crazy, ricocheting around the inside of the giant crystal globe with so much vigor that Candace started to stress about its "structural integrity." If the orb shattered . . .

Don't even think about that! Candace commanded herself. She had a poison powder to counter-catalyze by midnight; she couldn't be worrying about breaking historic monuments (albeit purely by accident)!

It was no easy task plucking the filaments, though. They were as slippery as a school of fish. As a bar of soap in the bathtub! Any time the tip of the remote-controlled tweezers got anywhere close, the motion-sensitive plasmatic electrodes would immediately dart to the opposite end of the orb. "Patience," Candace grumbled after she'd failed to grab an especially elusive blue one on the third try. "Patience!" she growled on the eighth. Frustrated, she stopped, and contemplated the big, beautiful, infuriating orb before her. She took off her glasses and sponged the sweat from her brow with the sleeve of her lab coat. The gesture reminded her of the kooky mayor with her ludicrous powderpuff. That strengthened Candace's resolve.

"Please, Lady SynchroniCity," she spoke to the statue again. "I just need a few of your plasma filaments. I've run a hundred different tests in the FLab over the past twenty-four hours, and the results are always the same: The only way we can detox BeauTek's powder is with a dash of this, mixed with a sprinkling of that. 'This' being the plasma, 'that' being the, er, whatchamacallit. Or the Whoseewhatsit, to be specific. Don't you want to help me and the Ultra Violets? Don't you want the citizens of your city to stay sane?"

Candace closed her eyes. She massaged her temples, which had begun to throb along with the plasma strands. "*OhmV*," she exhaled, hoping to ward off a headache. Then she put her glasses back on. And as her vision came into focus once more, she saw several glowing filaments wrapped around the tweezers. While it had hung motionless inside the orb, they had simply fallen into place.

"Oooh!" Candace pinched them tight before they could slip away again. "I've got you, my pretties!"

The rest of the operation was way less vexing. She angled the tweezers back out of the eraser-sized hole and then, spraying a fast-drying polymer embedded in its base, she vacuum-sealed the entire multi-tooled apparatus inside a transparent pouch. After she'd trackballed it through the window, she manually detached the extension—which just means that she screwed it off using her hands. It was only when she was holding the polymer pouch that she realized the tiny crystal disk was inside it, too, still stuck to the swizzle spork.

"Sugarsticks," Candace said. She wasn't about to open up the pouch and risk setting the filaments loose inside the cloudship—she'd wait till she was back in the FLab for that. But she couldn't leave a hole in the statue's orb, either!

She glanced around the aircraft that she herself had custom-designed, scanning the console and cabinets and overhead compartments for a solution. Her eyes fell upon a roll of something silvery.

"It's not perfect." Candace frowned, picking it up and putting it on her wrist like a bracelet. "But it will have to do."

Then, once she'd secured the polymer pouch for transport, she tore off a square of that shiny gray duct tape with her teeth. Reached out the open window of the cockpit. And slapped it across the small hole in the big orb. The filaments went frenetic all over again.

"I'll come back and fix it right, I pinkie-swear!" Candace called to Lady SynchroniCity as she zoomed the cloudship past her serene face en route to the FLab. The teenius felt certain that the statue's pink-and-green gaze shone with encouragement. "Just as soon as we pull off the Lilac Attack!"

Zowie

Code Name: Lilac Attack
Primary Aim: Poison Powder Plasmalytic Conversion
Objective Numero Two: Mutant Neutralization
And Thirdly: Black Swan Butt-Kicking

"That seems about right," Candace said, distractedly spinning the cuff of duct tape on her wrist while surveying the pie chart Cheri had calculated and Iris had designed. The teenius had been too busy to bother taking the roll off in the FLab; she'd been in such a rush there, dealing with the filaments. And then she'd had to jet straight over to CVUV to pick up the girls. By now she'd all but forgotten about her unusual new bangle.

On the illustration that beamed from one of the smaller screens inside the cabin of the cloudship, the three goals of the mission were split into three unequal pieces. The main aim, poison powder conversion, got the biggest slice—half the pie. Iris had aptly shaded it an unappetizing greenish yellow. Objective numero two, neutralizing the mutants, took up a third of the circle. Instead of making that wedge just one color, Iris had digitally sketched a warped portrait of Catfish Face inside it. The sight caused Scarlet to break out in a cold sweat. She'd yet to tell anyone about her Jack nightmare—it was only a bad dream, so what would be the point? But the depiction of the whiskered fish-face gave her flashbacks.

The remaining piece of the pie was filled with a feather pattern. Black on black, of course.

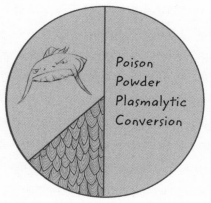

Poison
Powder
Plasmalytic
Conversion

"The only thing I'd maybe change"—Scarlet stared up at the infographic—"is to make the slice of kick butt bigger."

"A bigger butt?" Cheri weighed the options. "It *is* the smallest portion of our plan, but I suppose we could always prorate it."

No one else had any idea what that meant. Not even Candace.

The erstwhile babysitter spun back around in the pilot's seat and shifted the cloud into FLY. Slowly she floated the aircraft off the clubhouse's rooftop and into the windstream.

"How goes the rest of final prep back there?" she called, glancing up in her rearview mirror.

"Aces," Iris said somberly. The captured filaments, now contained in a quartz pendant about the size of a ping-pong ball, bathed her downturned face in ever-changing shades. She was standing over a foldout table like a war general in the field, a scroll of violet-colored wax paper rolled out in front of her. "These purple-prints that we drafted, based on the original blueprints we hacked from BeauTek, diagram the central ventilation chute on this so-called Bleau-Fryer contraption. All I have to do is . . ."

As Iris recited her part in Operation Lilac Attack, Opal looked over at her with a mixture of shock and awe. Considering all the day's work, maybe Iris couldn't find a moment to comb out the tangles in her hair from the Tom's Diner coffee jaunt that morning. But Opal suspected that, no, Iris just didn't care. And between morning and night, the knots had gotten infinitely more complicated, vining into thick, ropelike dreadlocks. Opal could swear that the lavender rat's nest had grown a full foot longer since their latte-fueled strategy session. Add to that Iris's electric-purple hummingbird wings, hanging from her shoulders like a glittering cape. The radiant plasma pendant strung around her neck. Oh, and the face paint. Escalating from simple eyeliner, Iris had gone and slapped a broad band of black across her eyes, decorating it with dots and swirls of neon violet. Lit from below by the ever-flickering filaments, the effect was absolutely fearsome. And ultra fabulous.

"Like a Maori warrior!" Candace had exclaimed when she'd first come down into the clubhouse with the plasmatic pendant she'd forged, while Cheri and Scarlet had both clamored, "Ooh, do me, too! Do me!"

And so Iris had, painting a blazing red bar to frame Scarlet's steel-gray eyes and embellishing it with black, then painting a hot pink swath on Cheri and highlighting it with bright green.

"C'mon, Opaline, you're next," Iris had said, just an hour or so ago in Club Very. It wasn't a question. Iris had dipped a brush into a pot of face paint, tapping off the excess on the rim. Opal had closed her eyes and clutched her sleeves. And now—she gingerly touched her cheek—she had a day-glo orange band across her face, accented with curlicues of pure white.

"Approaching Ground Gazebra!" Candace announced from the cockpit. "How's that primer coming along, Cher?"

"Très bien, I think!" Cheri called back cheerily, aiming a squeeze bottle over a large thermos of sloshing violet liquid that Scarlet was holding out at arm's length. "I've just got to add the Whoseewhatsit!"

"Remember, only a few drops!" Candace called back. "Because that Whoseewhatsit is—"

Before Candace could finish her warning, a blazing purple flame the size of an exploded watermelon burst up from the flask. "Hey, whatseewhosit?!" Scarlet protested as Cheri muttered "Oopsie!" and checked the chemical equation on her smartphone again—since what she'd squirted out was easily a dollop.

"Opal?" Candace asked, turning to look over her shoulder, turning the controls as she did so, and nearly sending the cloud-ship into a tailspin. "Ready for some superpowered action on the side of the good guys—or good girls, anatomically speaking?"

Just then they hit a patch of turbulence. Opal's stomach dropped along with the aircraft, and she gripped the armrests of her seat so tight her knuckles went as white as the warpaint on her face. "Yup!" she gulped through gritted teeth. She was flying around in a cloud, surrounded by three old friends who now looked like glam-rock kabuki robots. *The mutants*, she thought, *will be much less intimidating.*

"Here we are now," Candace said, coasting the cloudship to a stop. She flipped a few switches on the dashboard, and the entire cabin lit up with monitors. All four girls eyed the live feed, filmed by the MAUVe drone and beamed back to the cloudship's control panels via satellite. It was weird to see on-screen, in close-up, what was happening on the ground directly below them—like how it's weird when people in the front row at a concert watch the whole show through their camera phones.

"Ground Gazebra." Scarlet shook her head, the ends of her black bangs sweeping across the swath of red warpaint. "It's a crying shame."

"Seriously," Cheri agreed, screwing the lid onto the thermos. "Good thing our makeup masks are waterproof."

By now the Gazebra was long gone, save for the stack of splintered black-and-white timbers still off to one side. Huge mobile floodlights illuminated the pit where the pavilion had been. Despite it being almost midnight, the site buzzed with activity. An entire crew of mutants, all outfitted in their luau uniforms, swarmed in and out of the crater like ants at a picnic. In fact . . .

"They *are* ants," Opal uttered, getting out of her seat. "All of them!"

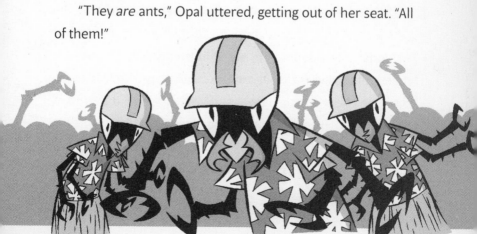

"Ants on steroids," Scarlet snarled, sizing up her opponents.

"An ant brigade." A shiver ran all the way from the top of Cheri's head to the tip of Darth's tail. "Eww."

The four girls ick-faced at the realization, and Scarlet instinctively covered the freckles on her cheeks. Objective numero two had been a mere bullet point on their battle plan. But now it was real. Itchingly, twitchingly, skin-scratchingly real.

"No sight of the Black Swans, though," Cheri noted.

"Probably past their bedtimes," Scarlet said with a smirk, although a small part of her was relieved. Have no fear, she was totally down with Black Swan Butt-Kicking. She could teach an online course on Kicking Black Swan Butt. If the essay topic on her English exam was "Describe in No More than 200 Words How to Butt-Kick a Black Swan," she would get an easy A+. That didn't mean she still didn't feel mixed up about the maddening Agent Baxter, who had both saved her life and bombed the Gazebra right before her eyes.

Plus, she had this little problem of a giant ant infestation to deal with. She could do without the distraction that was Jack.

Suddenly Iris pointed her rhinestone stylus at the far corner of the largest screen in the cabin. "Ultra Violets, there it is," she said, her pale blue eyes widening within the band of black paint. "The evil machine. The Bleau-Fryer."

The four girls fell silent. Twiddling at the control panel, Candace locked the cursor onto the apparatus, then zoomed in, increasing the size of the image umpteenfold. At the same time, on her iCanvas, Iris pulled up the matching digital files to the purple-print schematics she'd laid out on the table. With another tap on her tablet, the diagram overlapped the real-time image on the monitor, blinking a violet outline of the ventilation system Iris had identified. It moved along with the actual machine, which a team of MutAnts was hauling toward the gaping hole left behind by the Gazebra.

The hulking contraption was mostly circular in shape, like a giant tire knocked on its side. Or perhaps the world's biggest pie. Wide, curved vents opened on a diagonal across the top, this latticed metal crust exposing not a sweet fruity filling but the sharp-edged blades of the fans beneath. The back end of the circle jutted out in a cumbersome square. A tube extended from the front and narrowed into a nozzle at the end. Alongside the diagram, a description ran down the screen:

Bleau-Fryer: a motorized, ionized, pathogen-dispersal system with a box engine encased in a rear compartment; rotating turbines located in the central, circular cavity; and a barrel averaging ten feet in diameter and twenty feet in length projecting from the front. By combining heat and wind, the machine catalyzes condensed chemical agents, simultaneously transmuting and distributing the active ingredients. Copyright © BeauTek Industries.

"So"—Iris tapped her rhinestone stylus against the palm of her hand—"a ginormous heat blast is supposed to activate the mind-control agent in the crazy powder."

"And a ginormous wind blast is going to spread it through Sync City," continued Opal.

"It's basically just a stadium-sized blow dryer, isn't it?" Cheri concluded, absentmindedly smoothing back her sleek berry-red waves. Darth, peeking out from his papoose, did the same, passing a paw through the fur on top of his head so that the very beginnings of his purple stripes stood up like a tiny Mohawk.

"How darling!" Cheri cooed, beaming down at him. "Now Darth looks like a warrior, too! The most adorable warrior ever!"

With all of Sync City precious minutes away from being blanketed by brainwashing powder, it was not the best time to be fawning over a cute skunk, but the girls all paused to admire Darth's faux-hawk. Cheri would have given him a kiss on the head, except that would have crushed his updo.

"RiRi, that reminds me," she chanced, because Iris's hot-messedness had been bothering her all day. "I have the perfect detangling spray, if you want to brush out your—"

"Not now." Iris and Candace actually said it together: Iris with blunt determination, Candace with more urgency. "Countdown to Lilac Attack, UVs," the teenius stated. "You three got your wings on? Opal, ready for drop-off?"

Before she even knew what she was doing, Opal reached out and grabbed Iris's hand. Iris was surprised, but she didn't pull away. "No," Iris said. "We do it like this." And she held out her pinkie finger. "Shazam," she said solemnly, colored shadows from the pendant's filaments flitting across her face.

"Ka-pow!" Jittering with nervous energy, Scarlet touched pinkies with a lot more enthusiasm.

"Wait, what's my ironic superhero word again?" Cheri wondered, joining the huddle.

Darth squeaked something up to her.

"Oh, right! Blammo!" She giggled, anxiously nibbling on her manicured thumbnail. "I spaced for a second. What's yours, Opal?"

Opaline was the last to pile on to the pinkie swear. When she did, an ultraviolet mini-blast of lightning bolts and rainbows flared up from their fingertips. She blurted out the first word that came to mind.

"Zowie?" she ventured, blinking at the pink-, red-, and black-masked eyes of the other three.

"We'll work on it," Iris said with a smile and a shrug as the girls broke out of the clutch. And Candace opened the hatch.

23

Pluck, Eww!

OF COURSE, IF YOU ARE GOING TO INFILTRATE A late-night construction site where an evil cosmeceutical company is in the process of firing up a behemothic blow dryer, it helps to be invisible. Or at least camouflaged.

"This will only last a few minutes," Iris cautioned, tugging on one of her ratty purple dreadlocks as she changed first Cheri, then Scarlet, into sort of see-through versions of themselves, with just their bands of pink and red warpaint, their glowing hair, and their robotic wings a bit more noticeable. "Mostly long enough to get us down to the ground undetected. So we've got to, um . . ."

"Bust a move?" Scarlet suggested, circling in a spontaneous Harlem shake perilously close to the open hatch in the back of the cloudship.

"Yes, be fast." Turning her pinkie on herself and zigzagging it from head to toe as if she were spritzing on perfume, Iris was last to fade. But the ping-pong plasma pendant hanging at the hollow of her neck still shone bright. "The Bleau-Fryer coordinates are on all our phones. We go in—"

"You hit the machine," Scarlet parroted, the wind from the hatch fanning her now-aubergine ponytail above her head. "I hold off the MutAnt assault."

"And Darth and I are on powder patrol," Cheri finished, checking again that the thermos of liquefied Whoseewhatsit was sealed tight and secured to her belt. And then checking a pocket mirror to see that her lip gloss hadn't smeared. "But Scar, are you sure you'll be okay? That looked like an awful lot of mutants . . ."

"No worries!" Scarlet said with forced bravado. "I mean, there can't be more than, what, twenty of them? Piece of cake!"

"Or easy as pie?" Iris said, making an effort to kid around the way she usually did during a mission. "And by then, Opal should be on the ground, too, to help you deal."

"Right, Opal?" Scarlet hollered across the cabin. She felt pretty confident that Opal was on board with the Lilac Attack. But she wouldn't know for sure till they were in the thick of it.

The only one without wings, Opal had strapped herself back into her seat to keep from being sucked out of the cloudship's hatch and into the actual clouds. In her hands she nervously twirled one of Candace's swizzle sporks, which she couldn't remember picking up. Between the rushing wind and the whirr of the cloudship's engines, she had hardly heard a word Scarlet had said. She could barely even see her! All she knew was that a pair of steely gray eyes framed by a band of red and streamers of burgundy-black hair seemed to be glaring at her. Opal just nodded, hoping that was the right response.

"Then let's blow this popsicle stand!" Scarlet bellowed.

"What popsicle stand?" Cheri shouted back, getting more stressed. "I don't remember a popsicle stand being part of the plan!"

"No, that's what they say in movies when they're going to blow stuff up!" Scarlet yelled over the drone of the engines.

This was news to Cheri, since they rarely blew things up in rom-coms.

Candace called back to all of them over the cloudship's intercom: "Ultra Violets, let's save the movie trivia for later, okay? Now are we ready to—"

Before the teenius completed the question, Iris had turned up the speed on her wings. Raised her arms out to the sides. Given the other three girls a wobbly smile. And wordlessly tipped backward into the sky.

Opal knew Iris was wearing the robotic wings. She screamed anyway, it was so sudden.

"Veronimo!" Scarlet whooped, both fists raised high, cannon-balling out after Iris.

Her wings vibrating, Cheri—sensitive to Darth's dislike

of heights and the thermos of Whoseeswhatsit at her hip—made a much more graceful exit from the hatch.

Which Candace then closed up after her.

The girls flitted off in three different directions. Between the darkness of night and their near invisibility, even they had trouble seeing each other. After freefalling backward out of the cloudship, Iris closed her eyes and let herself drop, feeling the wind like water, surging against her shoulders and streaming through the hundreds of tiny vitanium-crystal scales of her wings. It was only for a second or three, but for Iris the moment felt infinite.

Opening her eyes again, she wrapped her wings across her body and flipped around to right herself, then gradually glid (*still how it's spelled*) down over the Bleau-Fryer. The busy MutAnts became clearer the closer she got, festering around the machinery, sometimes on two feet, sometimes on all six to crawl under it. Iris noticed that their hideous tropical shirts had—eww—four sleeves for four arms.

She landed lightly on top of the machine, just where the barrel branched off from the round central compartment, and hunched into a crouch. Slowing her wings to FLUTTER speed, she stopped to listen. She couldn't see Develon Louder yet, but she could hear her.

"Is it plugged in yet?" the president of BeauTek barked. "No?! Well, GET PLUGGING!"

"*Skritch-skrutch-skreet-sznock-sznick!*" The sound circled around the cavity of the construction pit: the sound of giant ants scissoring their pinchers in agreement with Develon, their boss.

Keeping low, Iris began to make her way toward the middle of the Bleau-Fryer, cautiously hopscotching from one metal strip to the next. Her fluttering wings lifted her a little with each leap. In the gaps between, the chiseled edges of giant fan blades flashed as the floodlights bounced off them. Out of the corner of her eye, Iris spied a wisp of red wafting down. Her first thought was that it might be Scarlet, off in the distance. But as the crimson tuft drifted closer, she realized it was just a frilly fluffula leaf. Momentarily mesmerized by it, Iris squatted down again and watched as the delicate leaf descended, light as a feather. It landed briefly on the same metal beam, right by Iris's feet. Then a whisper of wind blew it away again, into the open vent just to her side. And the instant the leaf touched the top of the fan, it split clean in half, guillotined by the static, razor-sharp blade.

Iris gulped.

"I said PLUG IT!" she heard Develon bellow. "CHOP CHOP! Let's get these $#&% turbines turning!"

With a shake of her natty purple dreads, Iris snapped out of her daze and started toward the center of the Bleau-Fryer again. The glow from the plasma pendant colored the beams as she crossed them. Her tinkling wings sent the faintest song into the slipstream.

A song not completely unlike the kind you might hear coming from an ice-cream truck.

Curiosity piqued and mouth watering, a MutAnt crawled up the side of the machine. On all sixes, it began to follow her.

From her cannonball plunge, Scarlet had arched out into a swan dive, then dropped-and-rolled into the tall grass bordering the construction pit. The powdery breeze off the Joan River tickled her nose, and she tucked her face into her shoulder to silence her sneeze. She wondered if Cheri was soaring over the sporous sludge at that very moment. She thought she glimpsed Iris on top of the Bleau-Fryer—identifiable by her swinging purple ropes of hair and fleeting winks of electric-violet wings. The gigantic ant creeping up behind her was much easier to spot. Impossible to miss, in fact. Scarlet nearly cried out a warning at the sight.

No! she warned herself sternly. *No screaming allowed! Leave the screaming aloud to Jack's nutjob mother.*

Stomach-down in the grass, she quickly scoped out the scene. It was dotted with MutAnts, scuttling back and forth in their bilious grass skirts, consulting clipboards and brandishing screwdrivers, yawping into walkie-talkies and nipping away at ice-cream cones.

Ice-cream cones?

That seemed odd, even under the very odd circumstances. Then again, ants *were* known to love sugar.

Okay. Scarlet took a steadying breath. *I've just got to fly over to the Bleau-Fryer and crush that superbug on Iris's tail. NBD!* Although she wasn't so sure just how *B* a *D* it might be. Now that she had a better look at them, she could see that the MutAnts were three times her height. The way their hard black exoskeletons reflected the floodlights, they may as well have been wearing suits of armor. She could only hope they were as fragile as eggshells.

Guess I'm about to find out, Scarlet resolved. She got to her knees, thumped herself in the arm for courage, stifled a second sneeze, and bowed her head—fiddling with the click wheel on the control panel to increase the speed of her wings again. But before they were even open, she felt herself being lifted off the ground.

"Gesundheit," a gurgly voice gluggled in her ear.

Sugarsticks! Scarlet cursed, squirming around to face her nightmare.

The catfish mutant gummed at the air with his trapdoor mouth, the gills on his neck expanding and contracting with each seaweedy gasp. From the gleam in his flat eyes, Scarlet guessed that he was smiling—or trying to. He couldn't turn his fixed, fishy frown upside down. But his rubbery whiskers flared out at the sides of his face, imitating a grin.

"Oh, eww," Scarlet retched. "Just . . . eww."

Hanging there in midair, caught in the webbed grip of a mutant, Scarlet's mind *jetéd* back over the events of the past few days. All the awkward encounters. All the tension. The stress of Opal's return. The shock of learning Jack was Develon's son. Of watching him blow up the Gazebra. And now a big bully catfish was mocking her. Slavering like she was his own little shrimp cocktail! All week long, every hop, skip, and *plié* of the way, Scarlet had managed to control her temper and behave herself.

Frankly, she was just about over it.

She wriggled and bucked, but her punches still fell short of the mutant, whiffing through the air. Catfish dangled her at arm's length. *As if I'm a bag of stinky garbage,* Scarlet thought, furious and flailing. *As if I'M the smelly old fish!*

Suddenly the sticky whiskers drooped down from their fake smile. And started to coil forward. Just like in her bad dream. Poking and prodding toward her face. Toward, she was sure, her freckles.

"Augh!" Scarlet yelled, completely forgetting about her no-screaming rule. Frantically she fought to get free as the sucking tentacles, and the gaping fishface they belonged to, leered nearer.

Scarlet knew what she had to do. She *soooo* didn't want to do it. But she liked her freckles too much to lose them to a mutant.

Grimacing in extreme ick-face, she reached out and grasped the moist barbels. They were even slimier and slipperier than she'd dreaded, like spaghetti coated in snot sauce, and she gagged at the way they felt in her grasp. But she didn't let go. She twisted and she tugged. Hard.

Harder than her mom did when she used to braid her hair.

Harder than the purple nurples Scarlet used to bestow on mean boys in the schoolyard.

Ultra Violet hard.

Yeah, ouch. Big time.

Scarlet squeezed her eyes shut, but she could still hear the whiskers ripping out at the roots with a sickening *pop-pop-pop* that made her retch again.

"Gleerck!" the mutant screeched in agony, releasing the superstrong supergirl at last. The force of her tugging sent Scarlet tumbling into the construction pit, plucked barbels still slithering in her fists.

"So gross," Scarlet spluttered, flinging the tentacles aside and wiping her sticky palms on the tops of her jeans. As the dust cleared, she looked down. And realized that dirt now covered most of her no-longer-invisible self.

Then—*"skritch-sznock-skreet"*—she looked up. To a circle of beady-eyed ant heads. And realized that she was surrounded.

Antics

"OH. SWELL. NO," SCARLET MUTTERED, GETTING TO her feet and dusting herself off, although doing so was beyond pointless now. Standing at her full height, she barely reached the top of the MutAnts' swollen abdomens—which, she randomly recalled from science class, were topped by thoraxes. "And these two segments are connected by a narrow node—like a waist," the drone of their teacher, Mr. Knimoy, came back to her.

That'll work, Scarlet thought, as the exo-helmeted black heads with their scissoring pinchers bowed down toward her. *It better!*

Spreading her arms out in second position, she bounced down in a grand *plié*. Then she sprung up into *sous-sus relevé*, her luminous aubergine ponytail slapping a few of the MutAnts in their compound eyes. One leg raised in *passé*, she began to pirouette, faster and faster, drilling up dirt as she spun. With a jump from just her supporting leg, she whipped out the other and, holding it at a near-right angle, sliced a neat circle through the weak waist joints of the MutAnts. Kind of like a can opener. One by one the monsters snapped in half, splitting into skirts and shirts.

NBD after all! Relieved, Scarlet landed in *petite changement*, then high-stepped in *pas de cheval* over the thrashing torso of one of the fragmented MutAnts. *Now, on to crushing the bug that's chasing Iris.* Once more she went to reboot her wings. But she soon noticed that they seemed to be damaged from her tumble, one of them bent backward like a broken arm.

She was concentrating on twisting the warped framework into alignment again when she felt eyes on her.

Thousands of them.

Thousands of compound eyes belonging to hundreds of

mutant ants, swarming around her like she was the last piece of watermelon on the planet.

"But how . . ." Scarlet stammered, glancing over her shoulder to make sure the batch she'd kicked in half hadn't regenerated. But no, that group was done for. The MutAnts now drooling over her were a brand-new crew. "But where . . ." she rasped, her throat dry with dust.

There were so many MutAnts, they seemed to be crawling right out of the ground. *Wait*—it hit her like a brain freeze— *they ARE crawling right out of the ground!* Before her vision was completely blocked by a sea of garish tropical shirts, she spied the giant insects marching one after another out of a crumbly anthill on the edge of the construction pit.

They must have a colony right under here! she realized, her skin breaking out in goose bumps. *I must be standing right on top of it!*

Scarlet didn't have time to be completely freaked, though. Because she had an army of mutant ants to slay. It was a BD. A VBD! *A deadly big deal*, she thought, gritting her teeth and clenching her fists. She'd been in some tight spots before. And she wouldn't go down without a fight. But she didn't have to be a math genius like Cheri to know that she was totes outnumbered.

"One . . ." Scarlet counted, executing a superpowered *sissone tombée* and cutting down the first ant in her path. "Two . . ." She toppled the second with a Charleston kick.

"Three . . ." The third one succumbed to a good old-fashioned sucker punch.

She stopped counting at fifty. She didn't stop fighting. But doubt and fear bickered like squabbling siblings in her mind, snipping away at her resolve as the scissoring jaws of so many—oh, so very many!—monster ants snipped above her. Cheri would be somewhere out over the harbor by now. Iris might be facing a MutAnt of her own atop the Bleau-Fryer. Candace would have flown off in search of the shifty mayor. How long could she go on alone? How would it end? Would she be overrun by the MutAnts? Would they carry her little lifeless body underground and present it as an offering to their queen?

"Never!" Scarlet cried, polkaing the next ant—approximately number eighty-three—to a pulp.

Another one immediately took its place.

With a yelp Scarlet tripped backward, recovering instantly in a breakdancer's crossed-leg flare to twin-kick the ant in its mouth. But its jaw sunk into her boot and held on tighter than a dog with a bone.

Sugarsticks! she despaired, yanking back her foot with such force that she wrenched the ant's head clean off. "Ugh!" she croaked, punting it aside like a soccer ball.

Another one immediately took its place.

If Scarlet had been a crybaby, she might have started boohooing somewhere around MutAnt number ninety-six. If not ninety-five MutAnts earlier. But Scarlet was not one for waterworks, not even under the most sob-worthy conditions. Scarlet was a warrior. She was growing exhausted. By now the scales of her broken wings were dulled with layers of dirt. Her band of red face paint was embedded with grit, her aubergine ponytail littered with the snapped-off antennae and torn mandibles of the many—oh, so very many!—MutAnts she'd dismembered. Surely she was doomed?

Doomed!

But she curved her back. Raised her arms high, the crystal discs of her damaged wings still jingling. And lifted one leg, preparing to crane-kick the ant directly in front of her, all the while knowing there'd be another one right behind it, when . . .

When suddenly the ants stopped advancing.

Oh, they were all still there. But they'd come to a halt. And ceased scratching at her with their hairy legs or nibbling at her with their jagged jaws.

They just stood there. Swaying ever so slightly.

"Scarlet!"

The voice sounded familiar, but she couldn't place it. Not Jack's. No, it was a girl's voice. Not Iris's or Cheri's, either. Scarlet wavered, locked in her crane pose, terrified that the minute she looked away from the ants, they'd set upon her again.

"Scarlet!" The call reverberated through the construction pit. "Dance!"

"What?!" Scarlet squawked, her eyes fixed on MutAnt number 104 (approximately), not even sure whom she was talking to.

"Dance! Dance anything! Just do it!"

Maybe Scarlet was too wigged out and worn down to think straight. Maybe dancing seemed like the best way to spend her final moments before an army of ants devoured her. Maybe dancing was the most natural thing she knew how to do. So she did. Hesitantly at first. Abandoning her crane stance, she rocked her shoulders back and forth in a tentative dougie, mumbling the song lyrics under her breath. "Teach me, teach me how to . . ."

"Now dance, mutants!" the voice commanded.

As one, the army of MutAnts did the dougie.

"OMV!" Scarlet gasped at the sight, stopping in her tracks.

The MutAnts stopped, too.

"Keep going!" came the voice. And at last Scarlet recognized it.

"Opaline?" she murmured, dropping down into a modest twerk.

As one, the army of MutAnts twerked their bloated abdomens, the fringe of their hideous grass skirts rustling with their booty thrusts.

Scarlet switched to some mindless prancercising while she tried to get her head around what was happening. Watching the ant troop gallop along with her every move, she almost began to relax. The whole scene would have been incredibly cool—if it wasn't so incredibly creepy.

A sputter of wind buffeted her swishing ponytail, blowing out some of the dead-ant detritus that had gotten caught in it. But this wasn't the mild breeze off the river, the one that had made her sneeze. This gust had come from the opposite direction.

"Zowie."

Scarlet jumped at the voice in her ear. (The MutAnts jerked right along with her.) She'd been so in the zone, leading what might very well have been the world's largest flash dance—certainly the largest one ever performed by mutant ants—that she hadn't noticed Opal skidding down into the construction pit to join her. Scarlet risked a quick sidelong glance. It was weird to see Opaline as the calm in the storm—instead of being the storm itself! She seemed a little lost, and yet not. Without wings, she reminded Scarlet of some clueless schoolgirl who had wandered into this midnight freak-showdown by mistake. Except that when you looked closer, you noticed she had a streak of neon orange painted across her face. And that wisps of white ran through the brown eyes it masked.

"Are you all right?" Scarlet wondered aloud—although it was hard to imagine how anything could rate as okay under the circumstances.

"Sort of." Opal attempted a smile. If she could have read the dancing Ultra Violet's thoughts, she'd have had to

agree: This scene was the apex of weird. She was standing in a construction pit side by side with Scarlet Jones, mind-controlling an army of mutants. "They listen to me, remember?"

"Right . . ." Scarlet switched to a bhangra routine, making all the MutAnts bustle like extremely uggo Bollywood extras, before asking, "But how do we get out of this?"

Opal thought for a moment. "Pied Piper style?" she suggested.

"What do you mean?"

"Well, the turbines are starting up—"

"I felt a gust!" Scarlet gasped again as it hit her. "Oh no, Iris! She's on top of the Bleau-Fryer! Right above the vents! With a MutAnt chasing her!"

"So . . ." Opal's silky brown strands lashed around as a second belch from the Bleau-Fryer blasted them. She stared at the shaking grass skirts and obnoxious tropical shirts of the monsters. "Let's do the conga?"

"The conga . . ." Scarlet repeated.

With a shuffle-shuffle-shuffle-kick, she led off the line. Opaline fell in behind. The MutAnts followed. And they began snaking their way toward the Bleau-Fryer.

Sk8rs Gonna Sk8

NOT THAT THERE'S EVER REALLY A GOOD TIME TO TREK across a massive blow dryer in the middle of a construction pit surrounded by a colony of mutant ants, but the worst time to do it would probably be when the enormous industrial fans kicked in. Something to keep in mind, readers, in case "hike across massive blow dryer" is an extracurricular activity on your next camping trip or an item on your scoutmaster's bucket list. You might want to *oopsie* "lose" the permission slip for that particular outing. Stay back at the base, chill, hoard the s'mores instead. Just a little friendly advice from the Ultra Violets. From Iris in particular, who at this very moment was making her way to the middle of an enormous metal pinwheel.

The first whir of the turbines took her by surprise and nearly knocked her off her feet. Flashing past the vents at her sides, the fan blades ground to life, slowly churning up to speed. It was as if a huge vacuum were sucking in the sky: The branches of the fluffula trees bordering the construction pit bent in toward the force, foliage and birds' nests and beehives and lost kites all dragged down into the vortex. The pull felt so strong, for a moment Iris feared for the moon. Dropping down flat, she gripped the rough metal edges of the beam she'd been walking across. Secure on its strap, the plasma pendant pressed against her neck.

Sugarsticks! she thought. The center of the Bleau-Fryer was maybe ten more steps away, but with those fan blades rotating below her, drawing in everything in their radius, it may as well have been in a foreign country. She didn't dare stand back up. To the swirling turbines, she was just another fluffula leaf. Iris liked smoothies—especially the triple berry ones at Tom's Diner. She just wasn't psyched to dive into a blender and become one herself.

Then, as abruptly as the fans had started up, they spluttered to a stop. "#&€$ing PLUG IT!" Iris could hear Develon Louder demanding.

In a yoga cobra pose, Iris chanced pushing herself up from the metal beam, just high enough to see what was happening.

From the back end of the Bleau-Fryer, the square compartment where the engine was housed, ran a stubby black plug connected to a thicker extension. In lurid BeauTek yellow, the second cord stood out against the green grass like a troll's garden hose. Iris tracked the length of it with her eyes, all the way over to the sidewalk, where she could see Develon in her pristine black pantsuit, her hardhat bobbling atop her silver hair bun. Scuttling around her, a smattering of MutAnts struggled with their multiple arms to hoist the extension cord's enormous plug and fit it into . . .

"Mister Mushee?" Iris mumbled. To get a better look, she stretched back a bit more, until she was kneeling on the beam. "The Mister Mushee ice-cream truck is BeauTek's mobile power source?"

The yellow cord didn't *quite* reach the Mister Mushee generator, a situation that was inspiring Develon to spew curse words in every language Iris had ever heard and many more she hadn't. Each time the MutAnt crew tugged too hard, the cord came undone in the middle, and they had to scurry into the grass to reconnect it. But as soon as they arrived at the hookup point, the MutAnts seemed to get distracted by something. Their antennae snapped straight, they stood on two feet, and they began shuffle-shuffle-shuffle-kicking in the opposite direction, off toward the front of the Bleau-Fryer.

This mutant mutiny only caused Develon to shriek and spew more as she summoned up yet another team of MutAnts to replace the one that had just meandered away.

Weirdness, Iris mused. *Could this get any more messed up?*

And that's when she felt the gnawing on her ankle.

"Gah!" Violet dreadlocks spinning like swings on a carnival ride, Iris whipped her head around and scrambled to her feet in almost the same instant. The MutAnt that had been hunting her all along rushed forward to meet her face-to-face, perching up on two legs, tilting its triangular head down, and reaching out at her with four wriggling arms.

"Eww, eww, eww!" Iris squealed, powering up as fast as possible. The MutAnt grasped for her glittering wings. Iris batted the four spurred claws away. And, prickly as burrs, they got stuck in her ropey purple curls.

"Quadruple eww!" Iris wailed through gritted teeth, violently ick-facing. "And quadruple ow!" As the MutAnt tussled to free its four entangled claws, it kept pulling her hair! To block its salivating jaws, she crossed her hands in front of her face and beamed out ultraviolet rays at random. Guarding herself like a boxer, she pondered her predicament:

I have GOT to get away from this monster bug! she thought. *But I can't walk blindly backward and risk falling into the blades!* She was already worried she might lose her balance just wobbling there, smacking aside the ant's grabby arms, which only seemed to get more and more entwined in her dreads. *Isn't it enough that it's so dangerous being a superhero?* she asked no one but herself, flailing at the creature as if they were in some silly schoolyard slap-off. *Does it have to be so RIDICULOUS, too?*

Squaring her shoulders, Iris tried to compose herself. Fists up, she stared at the MutAnt straight on, the stiff shell of its head sniveling toward her. With a jab of her right hand, she punched a blast of intense ultraviolet heat at its face, incinerating one antenna and searing a hole in its helmet. The smoking exoskeleton smelled sickeningly like burnt rubber. The ant screeched and teetered to one side, but still it wouldn't let go of her hair. *It can't!* Iris realized with shock. Out of the corners of her eyes, she could see that its claws were wrapped up in her knotted ringlets like flies in a violet spiderweb.

She raised her left hand, but before she could release another beam, fleshy teeth pinched her skin. The ant had sunk its jaws around her wrist like a damp, dull razor-edged bracelet.

Iris screamed in spite of herself, struggling with her free hand to scald the MutAnt's pinchers, wincing at the pain whenever she fried her own skin by accident. With just two legs and only one antenna, the MutAnt was quick but clumsy, skipping over the beams of the Bleau-Fryer, dragging Iris through the air like a chew toy.

It's going to bite my hand off! She began to panic as the frantic ant flung her over an open vent and slammed her down onto another metal beam. Every yank at her hair felt as painful as the first. Within the chaos, she fought for a moment of calm. *"OhmV,"* she breathed shakily and tried to assess the situation.

It came to her clear as crystal. Iris knew what she had to do. Like Scarlet before her, Iris *soooo* didn't want to do it. But just as Scarlet cherished her freckles, Iris valued her hand too much to feed it to a mutant.

Hair, she figured, *can always grow back.*

Narrowing the solar power streaming from her palm into a pencil-thin laser, Iris aimed at the middle of the MutAnt's forehead. At the same time, she focused her ultraviolet eyebeams into a pair of sleek scissors.

Sorry, curls, she found herself apologizing to her neglected tresses as—one, two, three, four—she snipped off the locks the MutAnt had clawed into.

She was almost loose. She just had to save her left hand.

The MutAnt seized and thrashed, trying to throw off the four natty clumps of Iris's shorn hair. But the severed strands, rather than unraveling, seemed to twist into chains. Instead

of freeing the creature's four claws, the cut tendrils bound them up tight as a mummy. Still the MutAnt held fast to Iris's wrist, wrenching her back and forth. Iris jerked around like a marionette, stumbling to stay on the metal beams, straining to sear off the monster's mandibles without giving herself sixth-degree burns.

It happened all at once. With a savage thrust of its damaged head, the MutAnt swung her up, out, and high over the blades just as, at last, Iris sliced off its jaws with a solar knife of violet-hot heat. And just as, too soon, the turbines started grinding again.

"Oh!" Iris cried, her wrist throbbing with fresh pain as the

MutAnt's pinchers tumbled away, exposing her raw skin to the cool air. She was vaguely aware that, beneath her, the bug had toppled into the blades. But there was no victory in the defeat. She was already beyond that.

Out of the frying pan and into the Bleau-Fryer. Iris stared from above at the mocking silver fangs of the machine and wondered why she always thought up such terrible jokes at the unfunniest times.

Feeling the suction increase, feeling the arc of her toss peak and her body begin to fall as if in slow motion toward the humongous fan that was beginning to rotate below her, Iris realized she was flying backward again. But now the wind wasn't buffeting her like a wave. It was drawing her down like water in a drain. If this moment seemed infinite, it was only because she was sure it would be her last.

With her good hand still scorching, she tore the plasma locket off the strap around her neck. With her hurt hand she managed to shoot out a tremulous rainbow. She couldn't be sure she'd struck the center vent. As she sent the round pendant rolling down the middle green beam like a ball in a pinball machine, she could only hope.

Hit or miss, the plasma was on its pathway. Now Iris worked desperately to open her robotic hummingbird wings. But her hands were too hot on the control panel. She melted the click wheel wherever she touched it.

The wings probably weren't strong enough to withstand

this pull anyway, she tried to console herself as she braced for impact.

Swish! She heard the blades lop off the ends of her longest remaining dreadlocks. *Krunk!* She heard them butcher the vitanium-crystal scales of her wingtips. She closed her eyes and sent out a final wish to the cosmos, that Opaline and Candace, Scarlet and Cheri and Darth, would stay strong and sparkle on without her. And then . . .

"Gotcha!"

An embrace.

The soft voice was barely detectable over the buzz of the Bleau-Fryer's engines. Later, when she reflected back on it,

Iris wondered if she had even heard it at all. If Sebastian had even said it. Maybe he'd only thought it, and she'd just sensed it, inside her head.

But in the moment, it didn't matter. The only thing that mattered was that he had caught her, and was zooming her away on his hoverboard.

"OMV, Sebastian!" Iris cried, throwing her arms around his neck. "You could have gotten sucked into the blades, too! We both could have been puréed!"

"Yeah." He shrugged it off as they soared out of the vortex's reach. "But I tricked out my board. Now *it's* turbo-charged! Those Black Swan dudes hooked me up with some sick equipment at that evil lab place!"

Iris lifted her head from his shoulder, a pattern of purple question marks breaking out all over her face. "Oh no, wait," she stammered. "You're not . . . ?" She thought she'd just been rescued. Maybe she'd just been captured.

"A spy for BeauTek?" Sebastian said with a laugh. "Nah!" He gave her a quick peck on the forehead. "Like I told you, Iris: I just wanna skate!"

26

The Pink and The Black

"IT'S A MARVELOUS NIGHT FOR A MOON-FLIGHT!"
Cheri said in a singsong voice as she soared above the river on flittering fuchsia wings.

A fantabulous nite! Darth agreed, peeking out from his papoose and snuffling the air. Although he did not really like heights, and he was not a huge fan of water, either, he trusted Cheri. So he tried to enjoy the view.

Were it not for her official mission to foil Projekt BeauTekification, Cheri would have loved to go for a scenic fly. Alas. It was as if the Statue of SynchroniCity had opened a velvet rope to the deep-blue, star-spangled sky. Flickering with aubergine and indigo filaments, her big plasma orb beckoned.

"Darth, look!" Cheri fanned a hand out toward the effulgent beacon. "Her colors are just like ours! And the plasma Candace took from her orb is going to catalyze those nasty spores! Lady SynchroniCity is on the side of the Ultra

Violets—yay!" She clapped her hands together, and the *whoosh* of her closing wings pushed her up even higher.

Cheri felt so buoyant, in fact, that she could almost forget she was floating over a harbor clogged with bubbling toxic sludge just waiting to be heat-activated by a weaponized blow dryer. For a lark, she swooped down on her wings and (*yes*) glid parallel to the water, like geometricians and swans sometimes do.

Swans, she pondered, scanning the muddy banks and reed beds of the river. So many shadows skulked in the dark. As she flew past, she thought she heard them whispering, and a frisson of fear shot through her for the first time that night. Breaking from her precisely equidistant trajectory, she surged upward in a folium-of-Descartes algebraic curve.

"Which is defined by the equation x cubed + y cubed - $3axy = 0$," Cheri said out loud into thin air to no one but Darth. "BTdubs." Something about the exactness of math helped calm her nerves. Math was straightforward and solid. Not shadowy.

Darth, however, was more interested in math in action. He tugged on a strap of her robotic wings. *Again!* he pleaded.

"You liked that loop-de-loop, did you?" Cheri teased, softly kneading the little skunk's silky ears—that always helped calm her nerves, too. "Maybe you're getting over your fear of heights!"

Rohlerkohster! Darth answered, holding tight to the sides

of his papoose as Cheri plunged and circled to one side, then the other, tying an imaginary bow in the night sky.

"I wonder if Scarlet and Iris are having as much fun as we are," she said, hovering upright within the hazy nimbus of the statue's orb like a hummingbird to a flame. She noticed what looked like a square of duct tape on its otherwise flawless surface. "And I wonder what Opaline's up to." From out on the river, Cheri couldn't see much of what was going down at the construction site. Lines of MutAnts, lockstepping in their grass skirts? Lots of them. Way more than the twenty Scarlet had estimated. But that was it. She couldn't make out any of the other Ultra Violets.

Iriz iz dropping dat bomb, Darth reminded her.

"So she iz." Cheri gazed again at the Statue of SynchroniCity's pulsing nerves of plasma. "Though the pendant is not so much a bomb as a . . . change agent . . ."

She trailed off. As she thought about the other three girls on the ground with the monster construction crew, she grew serious. Giving Darth a scratch under the chin, she said, "We'd better shake the Whoseewhatsit, right?"

Shake watz yr mama gave u, Darth replied with a giggle.

"Our mamas had nothing to do with the Lilac Attack!" Cheri giggled back. "They probably think Projekt BeauTekification is a good thing." She rolled her eyes. "Like everyone else in Sync City. Duh."

Dur, Darth seconded that emotion.

Just then, the first rush of hot air belched out over the

harbor. As it warmed the glut of spores burbling on the river's surface, they throbbed with a sinister glow.

"Uh-oh!" Fluttering in neutral, Cheri unlatched the thermos from her belt and twisted the cap to the SPRINKLE setting. "Now what was it Scarlet said again?" she muttered, flexing her fingers. "Um, veronimo!"

With Darth keeping watch, Cheri scudded parallel again over the sludge, shaking out the Whoseewhatsit like a crop

duster. Candace's warning had been right on: A little went a long way, spreading rapid as a rumor over the grellowy surface, staining it purple in concentric circles. And whenever the solution first touched the bloated particles, small violet watermelons exploded off the water, then disintegrated into powdery lilac-gray smoke.

"Pretty!" Cheri cooed at the chemical reaction. "Now when the *plasmafied* heat blast hits this stuff, it will be completely harmless!" But while she continued on, Darth spotted something odd. Darting through the muck behind them, a dim shadow was mimicking Cheri's every move. Its blackness blocked the next drop of Whoseewhatsit.

Iz dat a shark on a surfsbord? Darth asked, alarmed. *Iz it a swamp monster?!*

No, Cheri answered grimly, holstering the thermos and U-turning in midair to confront the threat head-on, *it's—*

A squirt of water caught her right in the eye.

Iz da Black Swanz! Darth exclaimed.

Don't I know it! Cheri seethed, blinking to clear her sight (and hoping the shot hadn't messed up her hot pink warpaint). Big Red Bristow had ducked back under the cover of his black umbrella, but there'd been no mistaking his tuft of carrot-red hair.

Furious, Cheri dropped down and flew directly at the darkness. Reaching it, she could see that the two spies, with erratic slaps and splashes, were pedaling a paddleboat. A big, black, swan-shaped paddleboat. Lil' Freckles steered in the front seat. Big Red pumped from the back. And both boys brandished Super Soakers.

If only Scarlet were here! Cheri fumed. Nobody but nobody could beat Scarlet in a Super Soaker shoot-out.

Diz wil haf to do insted. Darth burrowed snout-down into his papoose, stuck his butt out the top, and sprayed a gassy stream of bleu cheese–bellybutton whiff the boys' way.

"Urgh!" Big Red spluttered, scrambling to fan it back with his black umbrella. Lil' Freckles began to cough.

"A *Black Swan* paddleboat, boys?" Cheri taunted, placing one hand on the bird's broad plastic beak as she floated before them. "How adorable! What did you do, steal it from the petting zoo?"

"We decided," Agent Jack "Lil' Freckles" Baxter replied, pinching his nostrils and narrowing his glare, "To reclaim. The name!" He punched the dashboard of the swan-mobile for effect, then drew back his fist in pain.

"Yeah!" Agent Sidney "Big Red" Bristow covered for his cringing partner. "Black Swans don't just have to be doofy ballerinas! They can be cool spies, too!"

"By accepting. The label," Agent Jack argued in that tough, terse way of his, "We take back. Its power."

"Well, how very enlightened of you!" Cheri sassed, rolling

her eyes again—not that they could really tell in the dark. The spies actually had a point. But Cheri hated to admit it. She gave the tip of Darth's tail a tiny tug. *Again, please?* she requested.

Darth happily complied, dousing the Black Swans with a second dose of bleu cheese–bellybutton. The stench was so vom-provoking, even Cheri had to cover her nose.

"What the V, Cheri?" Big Red raged as a queasy Lil' Freckles ducked his head between his knees to breathe.

"Don't you boys 'what the V' me!" Cheri retorted, startled that Agent Bristow had dared to address her by name. "*You* don't get to say 'what the V'! Only *we* do!"

"It's. A Free. Alphabet."

Lil' Freckles's knees muffled his response, but Cheri still heard it. Hovering above the toxic Joan River at midnight, debating vocabulary with the spy boys in a swan-shaped paddleboat, she didn't miss the ridiculousness of the situation. *And we were having such a delightful evening!* she thought. Aggravated, she gave her magenta waves a toss and Darth's tail another tiny tug.

He pooted out a third cheesy stink grenade.

"Stop it already!" Big Red wailed, his eyes watering. "That stank is gonna make me ralph!"

"Get used to it"—Cheri paused to buff her nails against her shoulder—"because it will take days to wash off." Wishing once again that Scarlet were there with her, she gave the plastic beak of the swan-mobile a shove. If it had been Scarlet doing the shoving, the flimsy craft would have spun in so many circles that it would have caused a whirlpool. Cheri's push just rocked the paddleboat back and forth a bit. But with the added bonus of Darth's funky bouquet, even that seemed to make the boys seasick. Although Cheri could only see the back of Jack's salt-and-pepper head heaving between his knees, she imagined he must have been pretty green around the gills.

He haz gills like mootant, too? Darth asked, twisting right-side-up in his papoose again.

No, no, Cheri explained, *that's just another way of saying he's feeling ill.*

Darth arched a skeptical eyebrow at his beloved Ultra Violet. Keeping up with her expressions could be challenging, especially since Human was not his first language.

Cheri checked the time on her smartphone, then joggled the thermos. She still had a little bit of Whoseewhatsit to shake out. As the swan-mobile swayed to a stop, she decided to try reasoning with the nauseated duo. "Seriously, you dodos, just what do you think you're doing blocking my Whoseewhatsit?"

"Protecting his mother's investment, that's what," Big Red answered feebly. By now he was as pukish as his partner.

"And I suppose you do everything your mother tells you?" Cheri needled Lil' Freckles. "Even if it means zombotomizing an entire city? Or blowing up an innocent Gazebra!"

"She can be. Very. Demanding," Agent Jack groaned.

To Cheri, that answer fell as short as Lil' Freckles himself. She *tut-tut*ted in disgust. Darth *tsk-tsk*ed right along with her. Yes, she still believed in love, and she'd wanted to give Jack the benefit of the doubt. But she also believed her besties deserved the best. Scarlet was the strongest UV. She couldn't hang with a boy who was so weak. Too weak to stand up to his bossypantsuit mom!

"FYI," she said in defense of her friend, "contrary to what you may have heard, Scarlet is totally *not* hopelessly in love with you. And she never was."

"Really?" Agent Jack finally lifted his head up to look at Cheri. His skin was sallow in the moonlight, his navy blue eyes darkened with dashed hopes. "Not even a little?" Then, with a gag and a burp and a lurch, he leaned over the side of the swan-mobile and threw up.

"Wait," Agent Sidney interjected, as if Cheri's words were just sinking in. "This gucky stuff is supposed to zombotomize the city? I thought it was just deodorant!"

All four of them suddenly became aware of a heat wave. From Chrysalis Park, a heavy wind roiled out over the harbor, bringing the water to a kaleidoscopic simmer: exploding purple watermelons here, pulsing yellow powder spores there.

"The Bleau-Fryer!" Cheri cried. "It's bleau-ing!" Quickly she spun the click wheel on her wings' control panel, increasing their speed. "As much as I've enjoyed our chat, boys—one hundred percent not—I must dash, alas." She scooted around on her wings to face forward again. "Jack," she added, feeling sorry for the sickly Black Swan in spite of herself, "you might not be able to stand up to Develon Louder, but the Ultra Violets will. The Bleau-Fryer is a weapon of mass dumbification! I've got to finish spiking these spores before they're heat-activated!"

"I can't let you do that," Jack said in a listless tone, shakily aiming his Super Soaker. "I can't. Let you girls. Plasmatyze the toxin."

Frowning, Cheri looked back and forth between the wobbly boys in their swan-mobile and the slowly sizzling sludge. *Whatever are we going to do with these two?* she brooded. *We can't just leave them here as the river starts to boil!*

I callz in reinforzmints, Darth stated, swinging his head back and forth, too.

What reinforcements? Cheri repeated, puzzled.

And then she saw them: the trio of pink dolphins, swimming their way.

"Sine, Cosine, and Tangent!" she shouted, oblivious to the Black Swans' confused stares. "Would you do us a huge favor and—"

With a grand splash, the three dolphins leaped fifteen feet into the air and dove back down, their rosy tails flapping up a froth.

Alreddy tolz dem, Darth reassured her. And sure enough, without Cheri having to say or think a single thing, the three pink dolphins swam underneath the Black Swans' paddleboat, balanced it on their heads, and tossed the spy boys out of the harbor toward the park.

For those few seconds, the swan-mobile took flight.

Then it came crashing down in the grass very ungracefully and just kept going.

"Hey!" Cheri called after them, remembering too late. "Which one of you wrote the anonymous note?"

Only the dolphins replied, whistling and chittering like Cheri's question was a joke. She turned to thank Sine, Cosine, and Tangent, but they were already wading out toward the safety of the Statue of SynchroniCity. Cheri watched them leave, their three pink heads in perfect alignment just like synchronized swimmers.

Which was fitting, considering they were in Sync City.

Spy boys out of harm's way, Cheri made haste. Sneezing more than twice, she emptied the rest of the Whoseewhatsit over the percolating spores, then wished on a star that it was enough. Just in case it wasn't, she rummaged in her pockets, pulled out her bottle of biodegradable Lilac Attack nail polish, and poured that on top of the gunk, too.

"It *was* the inspiration for the code name, after all!" she explained to her trusty skunk companion. "Now let's go see what the other Ultra Violets are up to."

Blowing It

SEBASTIAN AND IRIS SITTING IN A TREE, K-I-S-S-I DON'T
think so. Not yet! Uh-huh to the tree-sitting, but nuh-uh to
the face-smooching. Not in the middle of the Lilac Attack! As
much as Iris might have wished for a first kiss from Sebastian,
as umpteen times as she'd daydreamed about it when she
should have been paying attention in history class instead, as
studiously as she may have practiced on a pillow, um . . . no.
Now was not that moment. She had yet to even allow herself
to admit the peck on the forehead had happened, because
she didn't want to lose her focus. Iris's mind was not on kisses.
This was not about boys! She had a mission to see through.

(Plus, her usually gorge purple curls were in a state of
absolute chaos, chopped up and dreadlocked and whatnot.
Sure, she hoped Sebastian would like her just the way she
was, but still. In her daydream scenarios, her hair always
looked perf.)

Now where were we?

Sitting in a tree!

Sebastian had chauffeured Iris up and out of the construction pit, over to a grove of fluffula trees far enough from the Bleau-Fryer that they wouldn't be vacuumed into its vortex. Iris had gingerly disembarked onto a sturdy branch, and Sebastian had joined her, balancing his hoverboard on his lap.

"Ouch," he said, grimacing when he saw the raw skin of her wrist where the MutAnt had bitten her.

"It's not too bad," Iris said, although it kind of was. "Except that I need my hands to . . . um . . ." she started to explain.

"To solar-blast the mutants, right?" Sebastian smiled and, right there in the treetop, peeled off first his hoodie, then the plain white T-shirt he was wearing underneath. Iris blushed royal purple exclamation points, but Sebastian was too busy fumbling with his clothes to make eye contact. "Hold this a sec," he said, tossing her the T-shirt. It felt warm. Iris wondered how it smelled. Before she could sneak a sniff, Sebastian had pulled his hoodie on again and taken the T-shirt back. With both hands, he gripped the collar and ripped the thin fabric at the seams. "It's old," he said. "And clean. Clean enough."

Iris swallowed, all at once aware of how thirsty she was. She could only hope the exclamation marks had faded from her face. Sensing she was supposed to, she held out her arm and watched while Sebastian gently wrapped a strip of the soft cotton around her wound.

"There." Sebastian knotted the two ends of the bandage together. "It kind of goes with your whole black-mask-purple-Rasta tribal vibe."

"Oh!" Iris uttered, raising both hands to her cheeks as they flared afresh with exclamation points. She'd completely forgotten she was wearing the face paint. She must have looked like a wild child!

But the cloth around her cut wrist did help dull the pain.

Lilac and yellow explosions erupting like popcorn from the harbor brought her thoughts back to the attack. Blinking up at her Graffiti Boy, her periwinkle blues brimmed with gratitude. "I've got to go," she said.

"I know." When Sebastian stared back at her with his shining black eyes, Iris doubted she would ever budge from the spot. She reached out and lightly brushed the forelock of hair off his forehead. It fell right into place again. "Can I help?" he asked.

"You already have," she told him.

Sebastian cocked an eyebrow. "Well . . . I'll be watching, just in case. Supergirl."

"Good," Iris said, her heart swelling like a balloon about to burst. Suddenly, even though her curls had been butchered and her hand had been chewed and her wings had been mangled, even though the Bleau-Fryer was heating up and Chrysalis Park was crawling with gigantic ants in ugly tropical shirts and at any moment toxic zombotomizing fumes could infiltrate the city, even though ALL THAT . . .

. . . Iris finally felt not only determined—she'd been determined all along—but optimistic. Inspired! It was one thing to fight to save Sync City for thousands of nameless citizens (and her mother). It was entirely another to do it for one special boy.

With strength and grace and her good hand, she swung down from the sturdy branch onto the grass. "Be back in a second or three!" she called to Sebastian, raising her bandaged fist in a sort of salute.

He waved double V signs in solidarity.

Then she ran.

Descending on her fuchsia wings, Cheri caught up to Iris just as she was approaching the brink of the pit.

"Hey!" Iris greeted her with a sweet smile that completely contradicted her battle-scarred appearance. She almost had to laugh at the vision that was Cheri: All ruby waves and glittering lip gloss, her friend may as well have just strolled out of a spa. "You're looking beauteous, Cher."

"RiRi, pardon my French, but you're not," Cheri blurted out bluntly. *"Qu'est-ce qui s'est passée?"*

"You mean what happened?" Iris guessed at the translation. "Tell you later." She could feel the undertow of the Bleau-Fryer's wind tunnel as she took a step closer to the edge, the suction tugging her frazzled dreadlocks forward. "Did you spike the sludge with the Whoseewhatsit?" she asked, raising her voice to be heard above the howling air current. "Is it primed for the plasmalytic conversion?"

"Yes, we think so," Cher reported, strands of her hair blowing into her lip gloss, as Darth nodded along. "Did you drop the pendant into the ventilation system?"

"Um, I hope so," Iris answered less certainly. Her mind flashed back to the ping-pong-sized ball of plasma rolling down the green beam of her rainbow. Had it gone into the chute? What if it had gotten stuck somewhere in the machinery instead of dissolving? What if it plum didn't work?

Darth clambered out of his papoose and up onto Cheri's shoulder while she checked the stopwatch on her smartphone. "How much time till it's activated?" she pressed.

"I . . ." Iris faltered, before throwing up her hands in frustration. "Gosh, Cher, I honestly don't know. It got kind of cray on top of the Bleau-Fryer."

"Obvi!" Cheri's green eyes goggled as she gave Iris another once-over, glancing at the bandage on her wrist before returning to her devastated hairdon't. "As soon as this is done, we are *so* giving you a comb-out," she declared.

"We?" Iris repeated.

Dont ezen tri to stops us, Darth said, folding his paws across his chest. Although only Cheri could hear him.

A heinous crunching sound caught their attention. Both girls crouched down low and peered through the long grass into the construction pit. What they saw made their stomachs knot up harder than Iris's hair.

Opal stood at the front of an endless line of MutAnts marching in place. The nonstop stomps of the hundreds of giant ant feet sent fissures through the dirt floor and dust clouds into the air. Every now and then, jutting out of the sandstorm, a wand of stainless steel glistered in the lights. As if conducting an orchestra, Opal was pointing at the mutants with Candace's swizzle spork.

For a sickening second or three, Iris, Darth, and Cheri all had the same tainted thoughts:

OMV, Opaline hasn't changed after all!

Sheez leedin da mootants!

And Scarlet's somewhere down there with her!

But as they watched for a fourth second longer, their pulse rates began to slow from panicked back to alert. Because as they watched, they realized that Opaline was directing the dancing MutAnts, one by one, up to Scarlet. And Scarlet, swinging a splintered black-and-white Gazebra plank as if it were as light as a wiffle bat, was popping the monsters into the air like high fly-balls. The cyclone of the Bleau-Fryer inhaled each creature into its churning fan blades. Shredded it like lettuce. And spat the gristly bits out of its nozzle.

That could have been me, too. There but for Sebastian and his tricked-out hoverboard… Iris shuddered at the thought.

"Yuck," Cheri muttered beside her, scanning the length of the line. It wound all the way back to an enormous ant mound. Iris followed her gaze, and both girls' eyes skimmed across the bevy of MutAnt bodies littering the pit. "What a battlefield!" Cheri exclaimed, ick-facing at the carnage. "Do you think Scarlet slayed all of them?"

"Yes," Iris stated simply.

Groz, Darth thought, peeking at the massacre through his paws.

For a fifth second more, Cheri and Iris observed in admiration as Opaline, with a flourish of the swizzle spork, commanded MutAnt after MutAnt up to Scarlet, who walloped MutAnt after MutAnt to its choppy demise.

"Doesn't it just warm your heart to see Scarlet and Opal playing nice?" Iris said to Cheri, a twinkle in her eye.

Cheri gave her a mischievous grin. "I'm so glad those two crazy kids worked it out."

"There's nothing like a MutAnt apocalypse to bring frenemies together!" Iris agreed, and both girls couldn't help giggling.

Verby funnee, Darth grumbled, skittering down from Cheri's shoulder to pace before them in the grass, *bud dis be going to take furever!*

Iris, although she couldn't hear Darth's complaint, had come to the same conclusion at the same time. The same time that the gaps in the ground began to look more like chasms than cracks. The same time that a dusky purple mist started to seep out of the Bleau-Fryer.

"The machinery!" Iris could barely contain her excitement. "It's overheating!"

"I see the lilac!" Cheri gasped. "The plasma must be melting inside it!"

Just then one of the chasms split off like a run in a stocking right underneath the Bleau-Fryer. With a metallic *thunk*, it slumped sideways into the breach.

"Scarlet and Opaline have got to get out of there!" Cheri cried, scooping up Darth and scrambling to her feet.

Iris straightened up, too. Her pale blue eyes met Cheri's vibrant green ones. "Are you thinking what I'm thinking?" Iris asked, an ultraviolet aura emanating out of her and enveloping both of them.

Cheri nodded briskly. "Darth," she said to the little skunk, "do you have any scents of the watermelon variety?"

Standing side by side on the rim of the construction pit, Iris and Cheri linked pinkie fingers. Iris aimed her free hand at the Bleau-Fryer

just as Cheri lifted Darth like she was the Statue of SynchroniCity and he was her furry orb. Using all her powers of illusion, Iris proceeded to disguise the ginormous Bleau-Fryer. From a dull gray, she turned the grid a golden brown, adding the sheen of a buttery glaze around the edges. In the vents in between, the sharp silver blades of the churning turbines took on a rosy tone, glistening with juice. Gone was the hulking machinery. In its place stood a massive, slightly askew, watermelon pie. As Darth began to spritz out the fruit's sugary scent, Cheri did the math, her vision filling with formulas, her hair glowing magenta pink.

"Curve your tail at a convex angle and rotate it on the horizontal, Darth!" she urged. "That's the optimal way to harness the wind resistance and maximize lift!"

Whaz?! Darth spluttered back, confused. *Whaz doz dat eben meen?!*

"Um . . ." Cheri searched for a clearer way to explain. "Just make your tail like a tiny windmill, okay?"

Dis I can dooz, Darth replied, shaping his tail into a purple-striped paddle and twirling it in circles to push his watermelon perfume down into the pit.

Picking up the fragrance of their favorite picnic fruit, the MutAnts started to spaz and twitch. Opal swept the swizzle spork and shouted out commands, but she could tell she was losing control of them. The air smelled sickly sweet. Purplish smoke was steaming out of the Bleau-Fryer. She looked over to Scarlet just as the superstrong Ultra Violet bunted a storming MutAnt off to the side. Scarlet looked back at her just as helplessly. The MutAnts were rioting: breaking conga formation and stampeding toward the irresistible watermelon pie.

"Scarlet! Opaline!" they heard the calls of Iris and Cheri. "Never mind the ants! Just get out of there!"

Right then the mob of onrushing MutAnts overtook Opal, tackling her to the ground. She covered her head with her hands as umpteen sticky insect legs trampled on top of her.

At least I'll die a hero? she tried to console herself. While MutAnt after MutAnt stamped across her back, her short life flashed before her eyes. She remembered the time she played a baked potato in the Thanksgiving play. The night she got slimed with the purple goo in the FLab.

The BFF ritual at Scarlet's sleepover. The chess date with Albert Feinstein.

Silly old Albert, she recalled fondly. He seemed as good a memory as any to be her last.

In a fog of smoke and dust, Opal felt herself rising above the rabble of MutAnts. She could see them below her, swarming on all sixes toward what looked like a ginormous pie. *Oh good*, she realized with bittersweet relief. *I'm going up. My apology tour must have worked after all!* But as the air cleared, she wasn't welcomed by a host of angels and pair of pearly gates. On the contrary, a very unheavenly holler snapped her back to her senses.

"Veronimo!" Scarlet shouted, skyrocketing out of the pit with a jazzy calypso leap. "Get ready to drop and roll, Opal!" And no sooner had Opal understood that Scarlet had carried her out than Scarlet lobbed her like a bowling ball onto the lawn.

"Zowie!" Opal yelped as she hit the grass and tumbled under the archway of Iris's and Cheri's linked pinkies. "And owie!"

Scarlet landed with a thud in front of her, all her superpowered momentum making her stumble forward several paces before she could slow down.

Opal shakily got to her feet, tugged up her knee socks, and stood beside Iris.

Scarlet trudged up behind them and stood beside Cheri.

"What's up?" she said nonchalantly, flicking pieces of ant from her aubergine ponytail.

"I saw Jack," Cheri confided in a low voice.

"Really?" Scarlet's heartbeat speeded up again. Even with all the craziness going down, her curiosity got the best of her. "Did you kick his butt like on the pie chart?"

"Pretty much," Cheri mumbled.

"And?" Scarlet asked, suspecting there must have been more to the story.

"And . . ." Cheri hesitated. "You can do better," was all she eventually said, while Darth reached out and gave her a comforting pat on the head.

Scarlet felt a twinge of disappointment. But if ever there was a time for boy talk, this definitely wasn't it. She stared down into the construction pit as hundreds of MutAnts spilled out of their colony to clamber up the sides of the biggest, juiciest, sweetest-smelling dessert they'd ever dreamed of.

And got sucked into the deadly guillotine turbines of the Bleau-Fryer.

"Is watermelon pie even a thing?" Scarlet wondered.

"If it isn't," Cheri answered, "it should be."

"We could add it to the list after hot dog cobbler!" Opaline chimed in with a joke. Cheri's eyes widened and she subtly shook her head as if to stop Opal from saying it, although of course she already had. Scarlet just flinched. *Now what have I done wrong?* Opal worried, feeling the nervous energy fizz through her. *The Black Swans are the bad guys—is it not okay to make fun of them?*

"Sorry," she susurrated, though she wasn't sure whom to or what for.

Iris's ultraviolet aura had expanded to include Scarlet and Opaline. The four supergirls stood in silence, watching the kamikaze MutAnts race to their own demise inside the pie-disguised machine as it tilted precariously to one side, huffing and puffing out great gusts of lilac-gray smoke.

"This is it," Iris said. "Pinkies crossed."

The purplish vapors were now so thick, they concealed whatever MutAnts remained. Which, from the looks of things, were none. Teetering around on her six-inch heels to the front of the machine, Develon Louder shrieked and cursed for an army that didn't exist anymore. She was stiletto-deep in their coleslawed remains—a fact she grasped with a furious ick-face of her own just as a burst of lilac fumes finally turned her pristine black suit . . . sooty.

Iris lowered her glowing hand, and gradually the illusion of the giant watermelon pie vanished, replaced once more by the lopsided Bleau-Fryer that had been grinding away all along. Within its machinery, the plasma-filled pendant had melted down to its timed release: A thick, hot, lilac miasma poured from the nozzle out to the harbor, where it blew smack dab into the congealed clot of powder, now primed for plasmalytic conversion by the Whoseewhatsit. As the wall of plasma-infused heat made contact, the sludge coiled into a ball—into a blob—on the surface of the water. A very big, purple-and-yellow blob, its surface boiling and popping with pus. Slowly, like a second moon, it rose above the river. It floated higher than the Statue of SynchroniCity. Higher, even, than the FLab. The girls gazed up at the strange, pulsating mass.

From his spot in the fluffula tree, Sebastian stared at the weird spheroid, too.

From the wreckage of their swan-mobile, Jack and Sid ogled the blinking blob with horror.

Hiking out of the crumbling construction pit in her seriously impractical shoes, Develon Louder was struck speechless, and swearless, at the sight.

"Coverage, anyone?" Cheri offered, opening her pink polka-dot umbrella, which Darth had passed up from the papoose. The four girls huddled under it.

For an instant more, the blob loomed there, far above the harbor, flashing yellow-purple-yellow, yellow-purple-purple, and finally, when the plasmalytic conversion was complete, just purple-purple-purple. Purple!

"It's like a giant throbbing brain!" Scarlet exclaimed in disgust and delight.

Then, with a sonic boom, it exploded, showering umpteen million lilac scintillas across the entire city. The harmless powder dusted the park's chess tables and fluffula trees, the tops of Sync City's skyscrapers, even the Statue of SynchroniCity herself.

Cheri couldn't resist. Hugging Darth close beneath the canopy of her umbrella, she spun round and round in the lilac sparkle-storm. Scarlet thought she was too tired from mutant–batting practice to join in—until she realized she was already spontaneously performing her own version of the famous dance from the old movie *Singin' in the Rain.* Opaline simply smiled. The moment reminded her again of that fateful sleepover, when Scarlet had showered them all with glitter blasts from her Super Soaker. She glanced over at Iris. Neither girl had to say a word. Opaline knew Iris was remembering the same thing.

Iris flung her arm around Opal's shoulders and gave her

a hug with her bandaged hand. "Operation Lilac Attack!" she proclaimed. "Woohoo! We totally rocked it!"

"No!" Opaline cried, so loud that Cheri ceased spinning and Scarlet came to a stop in arabesque. "Wait!"

"What is it, Opal?" Scarlet asked, concerned. She'd thought for sure that the worst was over. That she could finally, with her whole heart, trust Opal again. "What's wrong?"

"There's just one thing we forgot to do," Opaline said, her smile going sly as a crocodile's, her eyes swirling with white. Turning back to the construction pit, she pointed her pinkie. Took aim. And shot out a jagged, high-voltage bolt.

Blazing over the top of the Bleau-Fryer, above the grass, and right through the poster of ice-cream cone options, the lightning struck its target. With a final warped bleat of its eerie melody, the Mister Mushee truck burst into flames. Electric currents rippled down the extension cord and back into the Bleau-Fryer, scorching the circuits and shaking the frame of the giant machine. The tremors made the girls' teeth rattle as the ground gaped open and BeauTek's weaponized blow dryer was swallowed up by the sinkhole left behind by the MutAnts' vacant colony.

"Nice one, Opal." Scarlet slapped her a high five, just a little too hard (purely by accident). "Popsicle stand blown!"

xxvii

Sparkle Day

WELL, WASN'T THAT REFRESHING! HAD I MY DRUTHERS (have you yours?), I'd shower in lilac sparkles every single day. Not necessarily ones that had been poisonous perfume in a past life, but then again, beggars can't be choosers when it comes to combustible purple powder.

Since we're making wish lists, I also wouldn't mind my own pair of vitanium-crystalline robotic hummingbird wings, am I right? Perchance in a punky blackberry-gold color combo. Hummingbird wings would make my daily commute past the Statue of SynchroniCity *so* much more aerodynamic—and frankly, some days I just don't feel like riding my unicycle. Last—thank you for asking—I'd like a cheeseburger, medium rare, with lettuce, tomato, and pickles, please, but (and this is important) absolutely no onions. None. Nonions! NEVER! *screams unreasonably, shakes fist in fury at nearest onion tree*

I abhor onions.

Yuck, thy name *is* onions.

Onions, get out my grill.

Just who am I to hold such a grudge against onions, you ask? Why, I'm Sophie Bell, of course: the chick in charge of writing down these crazy Ultra Violet tales. As if you didn't know by now—I've only told you umpteen times before! (Okay, technically two times before, since this is book three. And two does not an umpteen make. I have a tendency to exaggerate. And to digress . . .)

You can bet the Ultra Violets were not eating onions at Tom's Diner the following Monday morning. Oh swell no! They were eating . . . c'mon, you know what they were eating. Must I *susurrate* it in your ear? Starts with a *P*. Rhymes with a "why." As in "*Why* is Sophie Bell rambling on about druthers and onions when all we really want to know is what happened after the Lilac Attack?"

Fine, be like that! And pass the ketchup.

"No. More. Pie." Scarlet pushed her plate away with a contented groan and slumped down in her seat at the diner, on the verge of a dessert coma. "I'm stuffed!"

"To the gills?" Cheri teased across the table.

"Ugh, no! Please do *not* remind me!" Scarlet put her hands up to protect her neck, laughing anyway. She'd battled so many MutAnts the night before that she could almost forget about Catfish Face. Once she'd finally made it to bed, she'd been too exhausted for nightmares. But if she closed her eyes now and concentrated, she could still hear the sickening *pop-pop-pop* of those slimy whiskers as she'd plucked them out.

Cheri, who'd been busy snapping selfies on her smartphone—and sneakily angling to squeeze that cute busboy, Philippe, into the background—pinched a stray blueberry off Scarlet's plate and fed it to Darth. As he munched on it, he reviewed their handiwork with pride. In the decontamination showers at the FLab, Iris's curls had been shampooed, and deep-conditioned, and slowly combed through until they were smooth and shiny and tangle-free again. You'd think that, after being shorn off by the blades of the Bleau-Fryer, her ringlets would have been shorter, or at least raggedy and shaggedy and all uneven in length. But no. They were as long and lush and riotously violet as ever.

Iris's hair was weird like that. Like it had a mind of its own.

Iris tucked one of the springy corkscrews behind her ear and, with a brand-new swizzle spork, speared a raspberry from the fruit tart in the center of the table, then dipped it in her bowl of lavender-latte gelato. "Mmm," she sighed as she swallowed the spoonful, smiling at her friends with her clear blue, non-black-lined eyes. All traces of warpaint had been washed off at the FLab, too.

"There's that grin!" Candace commented. "We've missed it, Iris."

Iris rolled those clear blue, non-black-lined eyes, but she couldn't stop smiling. "Sorry, UVs," she apologized, two small purple hearts blushing on the apples of her cheeks. "I guess I went a little drama queen there, with the makeup mask and stuff. I just . . ." She trailed off, glancing down at her wrist, which was now wrapped with gauze like a proper bandage. The strip of Sebastian's ripped T-shirt was stashed inside her messenger bag. She wasn't sure if she'd ever wash that. Eventually, she thought, she'd add it to her scrapbook, right beside the fragments of the heart-shaped balloon from her and his first date—because it *had* been a date, she'd decided, even if boys didn't like to call it that.

"It's so romantic how Sebastian swooped in on his hoverboard," Opal said, sighing next and stirring her swizzle spork in a figure eight around the scoops of chocolate and peach melba in her bowl. She wondered how Albert could

ever come to her aid. With the Pythagorean theorem?

"Romantic!" Scarlet scoffed, shoving aside her disappointment about Jack once more. "I'd call it kick-butt! Like in the Battle of Yavin when Han Solo and Chewbacca zoom in on the *Millennium Falcon* to blast away the Imperial TIE fighters so that Luke Skywalker is clear to shoot his proton torpedoes and blow up the Death Star! Though it's not exactly the same, because Iris had already dropped the plasma pendant before Sebastian showed up and . . ."

Now she trailed off as she realized that Iris, Cheri, and Opal were all staring back at her blankly.

"Seriously?" Scarlet said. Getting a second wind, she lifted her bowl of melted butterbeer sorbet with both hands and sipped right from the dish. "Not even you, Darth Odor?" she implored their skunk mascot. "Help me out here, little buddy. You're my only hope!"

I haz no idee whaz sheez talkin bout! Darth telepathically whispered to Cheri.

"You guys have *got* to see *Star Wars* Episode Four!" Scarlet declared, smacking the table in frustration. Their clattering bowls sloshed droplets of ice cream all over the place. "For real! It's a classic!"

Sensing an opportunity, Cheri announced, "Oh, would you just LOOK at that MESS!" loud enough for the entire diner to hear. "A veritable spill of ice cream! Howsoever will we CLEAN IT UP?"

Iris and Opal burst into giggles at Cheri's blatant flirtation—Scarlet was still scowling over their *Star Wars* cluelessness—but the dashing Philippe was nowhere to be seen.

"Alas," Cheri sighed in turn, just as the 3-D TV screens hanging from the ceiling all *fzzzzzt'd* with the official Sync City seal.

"Uh-oh," Iris said, shifting in her seat. Typically the TVs just played vintage cartoons with the sound off. Candace twisted around to look up at the nearest screen, too. The gaping face of Mayor Blumesberry goggled out at the customers from all four corners of the diner's front room.

"She looks like a gargoyle," remarked Iris.

"A goofy one," Opal agreed. She broke off a piece of the pie's chocolate-chip cookie crust and held it out to Darth, but the skittish little skunk ducked back down to the safety of his bag on the bench.

"Don't fret, Opal, he'll come around," Cheri said quietly, petting Darth's head beneath the table. "He just needs some more time."

Opal nodded, leaving the piece of pie crust as a peace offering on Cheri's plate. A hush fell over the diner's sparse late morning crowd. The mayor had begun to speak.

"Citizens of Sync City," she said in that same confidential, story-time tone she'd used at Synchro de Mayo. "I've called this emergency press conference to inform you of a terribly smelly terrorist threat . . ."

The mayor let the words hang in the air as all the customers in the diner susurrated with concern—some downing big gulps from their coffee cups, some pausing mid–syrup pour on their pancakes, some letting their frittatas go cold. Only the sassy waitress seemed nonplussed, chawing her gum per usual and not even bothering to look at any of the mayor's four faces.

"A threat," Mayor Blumesberry continued, "that's been thwarted. No worries, my peeps!" Then she split into her distinctive giggle, *"ah-tee-hee-ha"*'s cackling from all corners of the room.

"Anyhoo," she exhaled, blotting tears from her eyes with her giant powderpuff, "late last night it was brought to my attention that Projekt BeauTekification was actually—wait for it—a clandestine operation to poison the city!"

"Uh, a clandestine operation that you knew about all along," Scarlet snarked.

"Yes," the mayor went on, "apparently BeauTek Industries had planned to enslave the entire population by unleashing a toxic cloud off the Joan River." She winked in quadruplicate. "Can I get *what what*? You can't make this stuff *ah-tee-hee* up! But thanks to the diligence of my special security forces, I've put your taxes to work to save the day."

"Huh?!" the girls spluttered to each other. "WTV!" If Iris hadn't grabbed Scarlet's raised hand, she would have slapped the table a second time, even harder. Candace just frowned.

While the mayor nattered on, the 3-D images switched to footage of Develon Louder being hauled away in handcuffs from the site of the sinkhole. In her dingy pantsuit, deprived of the shield of her couture black Burkant bag, she looked like a frail ghost of her fearsome self. Gone was the hard yellow construction helmet. Her silver topknot had slipped to one side, and her face seemed to have sagged down a bit with it, as if the tight chignon had been holding it up. She ranted toward the cameras, squinting when they flashed, but it was difficult to hear what she was saying over the mayor's official statement. The girls only caught snippets of her defense: ". . . in on it, too!" And ". . . purse costs more than you'll make in a year!" And ". . . blame my son!"

Scarlet's ears perked up. "What did she say about her son?" she asked. The other girls shushed her so that they could listen.

The video showed no sign of the Bleau-Fryer. Or of the hundreds of MutAnts Scarlet had slain. Every last trace of evidence had disappeared down the massive sinkhole. Except . . .

"How is Mayor Blumesberry going to explain the lilac?" Iris murmured. "It's *everywhere*."

True that. Like a powdered jelly doughnut (to depart, for

a moment, from our recurring pie leitmotif), Sync City was absolutely covered in glittering lilac dust, glinting in the morning sun, fresher than new-fallen snow. Sanitation workers out in the street were sweeping it up by the truckful. School had been canceled for the day. The powder was too dry and flyaway to be molded into balls or igloos, but all throughout Chrysalis Park, kids sledded down hills of the stuff, or flopped on their backs to make sparkle angels in the grass.

The 3-D TVs returned to the live feed of the press conference, where a reporter was challenging Mayor Blumesberry's version of the events.

"Ms. Mayor," the journalist said, "there are widespread accounts that it was actually the Ultra Violets who stopped this allegedly terribly smelly terrorist threat. Several eyewitnesses describe a throbbing purple blob rising above the Joan River at midnight—and exploding! And that's why lilac sparkles are blanketing Sync City this bizarre Monday!"

Mayor Blumesberry gave one of her patented giggles, though Iris thought she detected more nervousness than usual running through it. "We all know little girls love their sparkles!" The mayor dismissed the reporter with a wave of her powderpuff. "But . . . no comment."

"Excuse me? 'Little girls love their sparkles'?" Cheri repeated with disdain while she freshened up her glittery lip gloss. "How condescending!"

"I'd like to sparkle her," Scarlet hissed, aware that the

other customers were stealing looks at them. "Right upside the head!" She began vogueing her arms in elaborate maneuvers, imagining a fierce new dance she just might call the Sparkle Smack.

As the Q&A session continued, with the mayor "no commenting" on every question about either the Ultra Violets or the mysterious lilac sparkles, the girls turned back to their celebration brunch. The mixed-berry pie was mostly gone. What remained of their sorbets and ice creams had liquefied in the bottoms of their bowls. Iris hoped the sassy waitress would swing by soon: She was craving a real latte, and not just the gelato kind.

"Develon Louder may be off to prison," Candace said, peering at the TVs through her thick black glasses. "But it's pretty clear we have a new nemesis on our hands. The mayor's alibi for last night is airtight: She hosted a midnight screening of the new *Wonder Woman* movie! Tons of people saw her—*not* at the harbor."

"It's like she set up Develon, knowing that we'd stop her! I can't believe I stressed so much about us coming out to the public"—Iris shook her head, her tendrils bouncing in all different directions—"only to have Mayor Blumesberry take credit for our, um . . ."

"Derring-dos?" Opal suggested.

"Yeah!" Scarlet slinked both hands above her head like a snake charmer. "Those!"

The diner's door jingled, though the girls didn't take much notice of it—until Opal realized the rest of the customers seemed distracted by something *not* on the screens and *not* them, either. Picking up the lingering stench of pungent cheese and bellybutton lint, she stifled a gasp. "Scarlet," she tried to warn her friend, but it was already too late. In full choreography mode, Scarlet swung her arm out swiftly to one side—and supervogued Agent Jack Baxter square in the stomach.

Scarlet's eyes popped open and she covered her mouth in shock, not sure whether to cry out or laugh. Jack doubled over in pain, never uttering a sound. Not an *oof!* nor an *owie!* nor an *ergh!* Behind him, Agent Sidney Bristow stood solemn as a bodyguard.

Both boys, head to toe, were coated in lilac.

Big Red's frizzy flattop was like a powdered lilac wig. Lil'

Freckles's freckles looked more like sequins, his previously salt-and-pepper hair an enchanting mix of dark grape with lavender highlights.

"Got caught in the shower, boys?" Candace said, struggling to keep a straight face.

"Now *that*," Iris marveled, "is an extreme makeover."

Leaping out of her seat and flashing the V sign in front of the stony-faced twosome, Cheri snapped some more selfies. "Should we start calling you the *Lilac* Swans?" she quipped. "Do you want to reclaim that name, too?"

Across the table, Scarlet shot Cheri a pleading glance to shut up. She couldn't quite explain it—and she definitely couldn't say it with him standing right there—but she sort of felt sorry for Jack. She'd watched him blow up the Gazebra with her own eyes. And yes, he'd tried to stop Cheri from priming the sludge with the Whoseewhatsit. But his mom, who was bat-poop bonkers to begin with, was probably going to jail. And, oh yeah, he was the color purple!

Jack and Sid tolerated the teasing stoically. Soon enough, Cheri felt guilty about it herself. The spy boys had been brats, but she knew it wasn't gracious to gloat. She sat back down with the rest of the girls, waiting to hear what The Swans Formerly Known as Black had to say.

Recovered from the gut-punch, Jack stood military-straight. And held out a lilac hand to Scarlet.

Scarlet's face flushed as red as the strawberries in the

fruit pie. She could feel the eyes of all the other girls on her. This was so embarrassing! The gentle jab of Iris's elbow nudged her in the side. Wrinkling her nose with doubt, she stuck out her hand, too.

"You are. A worthy. Adversary, Scarlet Jones," Agent Jack said in that strange, stilted way of his, pumping her hand up and down with a firm grip. "Very. Impressive. The way you neutralized. Those mutants."

Scarlet's Ultra Violet instinct was to yank her hand back and hurl Jack across the diner like a shot put. It took all her powers of self-control not to do that, and to keep her arm noodly-limp instead. But she had no idea what she was supposed to say! Any second now her palm might start getting sweaty. Her bangs were in her face, and her nose had begun to itch, but she couldn't do anything except stare back into Jack's (thankfully not lilac but still) navy blue eyes. She searched them for an explanation. All she saw were tiny lilac flecks in his lashes.

"Why . . . ?" she stammered, but her voice came out as a rasp and she had to clear her throat. "I don't understand why first you . . . and then you . . ." she tried again, but words failed her.

"Extenuating"—as Jack said it, Agent Sidney clapped a heavy hand on his shoulder—"circumstances. Beyond my control."

"Okay, bro, you shook hands with your opponent—happy?" Big Lilac said. "Now let's get out of here. After all night in the police station, I need to wash this purple stuff off! And that skunk stank, too!"

Agent Jack finally let go of Scarlet's hand. It felt numb. And it was covered in lilac dust.

"Later, girls!" Big Lilac bellowed, wagging his tongue at the table. Then he leaned over Opal, who shrunk back in alarm. "Later, traitor!" he snarled just at her. And picked up the last piece of pie before steering Jack toward the jangling door.

You want to wash off the purple stuff? Opal bolted to her feet, furious, and thunder boomed inside the diner before she was even aware that she'd thought it. A milky film swam across her eyes, and her hair snapped to attention, each strand a live wire. *Then get wet!* With a twist of her fingers, a charcoal-colored cloud formed directly above the boys, and a sudden torrent of water rained down on them. It didn't rinse away the lilac glitter. But it did drench their dirty suits. And soak their socks from heel to toe.

Agent Jack just gritted his teeth at this final indignity and squelched out of the diner. Agent Sidney stomped through the puddles behind him.

"Wait!" Cheri cast a nervous glance at electrified Opal as she shouted after the Swans, remembering too late again. "Which one of you sent the text?"

"The pie, *c'est finit*, mademoiselle?" came a voice over her shoulder. Cheri froze in place. Philippe had at last shown up at the table—and she found herself speechless. She just gaped at the charming busboy, who gave her a wink while he wiped down the table and loaded up a tray with their plates. "Ice cream for breakfast," he observed, nodding his approval. "Very decadent." Then he was gone.

Cheri released her breath with a faint whimper. She'd been holding it the whole time. "D'oh!" she blurted out to the other girls, and they collapsed into giggles. Even Opaline, whose storm had passed.

They were still giggling as the sassy waitress sashayed over to them. When she reached the booth, she made a big show of totaling up the bill on her notepad. Her Oreo bouffant quivered with every new addition. She finished with a grand flourish of her pen, ripped off the page, and slapped it facedown in front of Cheri.

"Because you're the numbers gal—right, Red?" she said. Then, with a curtsy to Scarlet, she spun a single pirouette in her orthopedic sneakers before strutting away.

"Red?" Cheri uttered as she turned over the bill. Her green eyes lit up with surprise, and she passed it across the table. Scarlet stared at the smiley-face zero in the center of the page. And then at the note the waitress had scribbled beneath it:

Sorry about the Gazebra, girls! But thanks for saving the day!

"The sassy waitress?" Scarlet muttered as she and Cheri followed Candace, Iris, and Opal toward the exit. "*She's* the one who sent us the anonymous text? *And* she knows ballet?"

Cheri was too busy looking over her shoulder for a busboy to respond.

Outside, in the purple-tinted light of day, the girls lingered a moment longer, not yet wanting to say good-bye.

"Back to the FLab this afternoon?" Cheri asked Candace, who was keying some code into her smartphone.

"Yes," the junior scientist said. "I'm *supposed* to be analyzing the chemical composition of the lilac dust for your moms—ha-ha. But since, of course, I already know that, I plan to do a little spying on Mayor Blumesberry instead. I'm just setting the coordinates on the MAUVe drone for City Hall now. How about you all?"

The four girls exchanged glances, then chorused, "Power nap!"

"And I'll probably do my nails after," Cheri added, giving Darth one last hug as she prepared to pass him over to Iris to bring back home to Club Very. "Time for a new shade. I'm plum out of lilac!"

"If I can get one of my brothers to take me, I might go night-sledding in Chrysalis Park." Scarlet kicked up a pile of the pale flakes. "Opal," she said, tracing her toe in the powder, "do you want to come with?"

"Really?" Opal clutched the cuffs of her dress to contain her excitement. "Um, sure, okay! How about you, Iris?"

Iris smiled at her three best friends, together again. She smiled at Candace, their trusty teenius. She smiled up at the sun, her favorite star, and her pupils got so small that her eyes appeared pure blue. "That would be so fun," she said. "But I have a super-important art project I want to get started on right away. A brand-new pair of vitanium-crystal wings to make. I'm thinking the colors will be pearly white and fiery orange. How does that sound, Opaline?"

Opal was so thrilled by the thought of her very own set of hummingbird wings that her hair stood on end again.

"Sounds viomazing!" Scarlet answered for her, springing into a joyous split. "Sounds like . . ."

Iris, Cheri, Opaline, and Candace all gathered around the smallest Ultra Violet, who grinned back at them gleefully as she said, ". . . like it's time for a dance!"

Candace switched from her drone program to her camera phone as the four girls lined up on the sidewalk in front of Tom's Diner. Opal didn't really know the words yet, or the steps, but they were easy enough, so she did her best to follow along as Cheri started them off with, "Ultra Violets ready and . . ."